BARRY'S WAY

96.858% TRUE
3.142% UNTRUE

SOME PEOPLE AND COUNTRIES NOT CORRECTLY NAMED FOR SECURITY

COVER

Photograph of a hammer kindly given on my birthday by Christina. It enables me to hammer home difficult facts and figures and keeps the pie in the sky box less full.

FOREWORD BY:

Councillor Richard J Edis Runnymede Borough Council

It is with immense pleasure that I have been given the opportunity to write a Foreword to this fine book written by Barry Pitt. Barry holds a Fellow Membership status in the Institution of Building Services Engineers and is a man of considerable ability.

I first met Barry when he joined me as a fellow Councillor on Runnymede Borough Council. He was always ready to help others, ask questions and seek answers for his residents.

Complex engineering problems have always been a challenge for Barry, and I think of him as an Isambard Kingdom Brunel of our time.

I found this book made interesting reading and wish him every success.

AND

Carol Quantrell
Past and Present Employee

I first got to know Barry when I was employed by BPA as a Secretary in 1984.

He was an extremely generous employer and treated his staff exceptionally well but expected the workload and deadlines to be carried out with great precision.

While typing this book some of the stories Barry has told have brought back happy memories.

PREAMBLE

Most 75+ year olds who are in reasonable physical and mental health who I know are quite forgetful – not remembering what to take with them until after shutting the front door, and why did I come into this room? From what I can make out, this is normal.

When considering 75+ years of active life and recalling all interesting moments it is quite difficult to state the particular year of an event, but I get there in the end, quite often by referring to other people who may know about or were part of the particular event.

Some of my recalled events are strange to say the least and my sons are not convinced some even happened!

A considerable proportion of those that were there at the time have sadly passed on resulting in many hours now being necessary trying to prove what I say is true.

I have decided to allow the doubters to consider some events such PIE IN THE SKY – hence the title of this book includes the first decimal places of pie and allows 3.142% of events to be untrue to those who prefer it that way!

PREFACE

I counted 37 'friends' who I thought would pay me not to be in my book, this was the reason I am writing it. It has turned out that most would pay to be in my book. So, status quo.

CONTENTS

1942 Onward	Page 6
2019	Last few pages
Appendices	Before Odds and Sods and Definitions
Odds and Sods and Definitions	After Appendices

1942

"Bloody well do something about it!" my Father shouted at Doctor Findly who thought he was about to be picked up, he had just brought me into the world but dead so wrapped me in newspaper and placed me on the bay windowsill – "Get me a bowl of hot and another of cold water quick" the Doctor ordered – my Father in turn instructed my Grandma called Nana to get them – all this as told by my Father later in life and remembered by my Mother.

This was the only time my Father swore. Both I and my family are quite sure this was the only time!

The result of hot-cold-hot-cold dipping brought me to life, and I was then declared a 'blue baby'.

I think this problem is now called Methemoglobinemia, back then in 1942, I am told that the treatment was "NO MILK" just Brandy and warm water for 2 weeks and then add the smallest amount of milk, gradually changing over to full milk over several weeks – nobody can remember how many weeks were involved. Not too keen on Brandy now, not sure why.

Just to add to the picture my Father was over 6'-0" and the Doctor who was a little shorter and thought he was going to be in trouble, as he was shouted at by my Father.

The family were adamant that this was the only time my father swore, and I can confirm this as well. Not like my Mother who was often heard using the word damn. I recall spilling something on the carpet and instead of asking me to get a prag she said go and get a damn prag.

1944

My Mum and Dad were strong followers of Sir Winston Churchill.

They chose my middle name as Winston, but according to family members the Vicar at my christening, christened me Barry Churchill Pitt. When the mistake was pointed out he did it all again.

(I am perhaps wrongly advised that the first and only name given at a Christening is the name you should be known as. I am, however, known as Winston not Churchill). Perhaps I am living a big sin!

1945

My Mother was due to give birth to my Sister – apparently the doctor was going to bring the baby in his black bag.
I needed to know more about this so I tied some string across the stairs such that the doctor would trip up and on falling, his bag would open, and I would be the first to see my Sister.

It didn't work.

The Second World War was still ongoing when I was 3. I was evacuated to Harlow in Essex just before the War ended in September 1945 and stayed with my Father's family who had 2 children, ages about 7 and 8. They used to put me in an old tin container and roll me down a hill – I hated it and looking back it must have been quite dangerous. After 2 weeks my Mother and Father came to collect me (my Father borrowed a company van) to take me home.

I clearly remember an iron construction in a downstairs room in Brancaster Road with perhaps a ¼" thick steel roof supported on 6 legs, each 3" x 2" angle iron with wire mesh sides 3' – 0" high. When there was an air raid warning, my Mother would take me into this shelter. We would wait there until there was another blast on the siren to let us know the air raid was over.

1947

I started school. I and Brian started together in Miss Snowman's class. I was given the dry sand pit to play with and Brian had the wet sand - whilst he could make sand pies, I couldn't make anything – my sand just fell flat. I was not pleased. I was going to spend my life getting rid of dry sand trays in every school. I haven't done very well.

A fireman comes in my bedroom window and carries me down a ladder into the back garden – great excitement – and then another fireman arrives with my little armchair. I was to sit in it and not to move. I don't remember my Mother being around, but no one was injured.

I understand some hot coal had somehow fallen out of the stove and set the carpet on fire. All my toys were safe on the 3rd floor.

1948

It was almost ½ mile walk to school, but it used to take ½ hour together with Scot another local boy – we played marbles along the gutter. The result was Scarlet Fever.

I was put to bed and my Mother had to nail sheets all around the walls and keep them sprayed with something all the time. My Father was not allowed into my room at all. She wore gloves when giving me my food! Whilst I was ill, May and Baker brought a new magic tablet onto the market called M&B tablets – these were I understand the first antibiotics and I was prescribed them, everybody was told about these exciting pills. I was better in a week or so and the sheets came down. I was banned from getting my nose close to drain grids in the gutter. Good job my Mum did not see me going to and from school, as I reckoned that with these new magic pills it wouldn't matter if I got ill again.

You need to know that my Mother used to call a fart a 'whisper'.

It was Sunday and I had to go with my Mum and Dad and my sister, who was 2, to a family afternoon – I don't know what it was in connection with, but my Father told me a little story and asked me to go and tell Nana by whispering into her ear. UNBELIEVABLE! – How could I do this – I told my Dad this was not possible, but I can't remember the actual words used. My Dad got a bit upset that I didn't do it – I didn't know why.

When on holiday in St Oseth, Uncle Thorn used to take the boat with a 'seagull' outboard motor along the coast about a mile to the village store. I always wanted to go with him, and did, twice I think.

1949

At school we are going to learn to write more words and then soon after we are going to learn to write in ink.
Each of our desks had 2 separate hinged tops, 2 seats and 2 ink wells.

I got very jealous that I was never appointed to be ink monitor. The ink monitor had to pour a measured amount of water into a special shaped 'tin' can and add 2 scoops of ink powder.

The mixture was stirred I guess but I never saw this process – then our ink wells were filled from the can which had a long spout. The ink monitor had to get right down to see when the wells were half full – that's all you were allowed.

We were issued with a pen and a nib – we had to slide the nib onto the pen holder and wow – we were away writing in ink! We were not allowed to touch the nib nor write on our arms.

Any talking or constantly getting this wrong resulted in a price of chalk being thrown at us at great speed. It depended where it hit but could be a little painful.

When a little older 3 or 4 chalks thrown resulted in a ruler suddenly hitting me (us) across the knuckles – that did hurt!
I must admit, I have the year wrong, I think the chalk throwing started in 1953.

1950

Once a week, Mum used to give me 2 little pieces of pink paper (about 5/16" or 8mm square). These were ration coupons and allowed me to stop at the sweet shop and buy 2 gobstoppers or other sweets, such as black jacks, on the way to school. They were precious and were carefully looked after.

My father had a very small extra job helping to make spectacle frames. He used to ask me to walk to the station and buy 3 or 4 newspapers for the craftsmen – we had a choice of Star, News or Standard, I think they were 1 ½ pence each.

If extra lenses became available they would be given to me, and I would be able to make a telescope with two cardboard tubes. Even the moon looked larger, it was brilliant.

We used to holiday in St Oseth borrowing a large rather nice hut built virtually on the beach. I had a kid's fishing rod and could easily catch eels. I loved chasing my Mum and Mary with a live eel – they used to be very cross. When the tide went out, we used to dive under the hut (it was built on wooden posts about 800 mm high and bring out the cockling rakes.

Off we went to the water's edge and started raking, loads of cockles would surface. We picked them up and filled ½ bucket, this being enough for us tonight although we could probably fill 2 or 3 buckets if we really tried.

At twilight my Father and Uncle Thorn used to go skate spearing. I went with them once, but we did not see any skate. So, my report is what I was told.

Apparently, they would quietly row out into the mouth of the River Stour, sit still, and watch for ripples about 2 feet (600 mm) apart. The space between was most likely a skate floating at the surface of the water.

I am told they would work out where its eyes were and shine a torch on them. This mesmerised him/her and allowed the guys to spear it and get it into the boat for supper tomorrow.

If we were going fishing the next day, forks (garden type) would come out from under the hut and off we would go worming.

Down by the sea you would look for little piles of sand shaped like strands of spaghetti – this means there is probably a rag worm underneath – just dig it out and put it into our Micky Mouse bucket. Half a bucket full would be fine.

Ordinary looking worms are called lug worms. All the worms are normally 8 or 9 inches long!

1951

My Father kept chickens; he had four girls and one fellow called Tom. Tom had his own little run and house separate from the girls. I can't remember why but Tom was very irritable and would bite us if you were daft enough to try and stroke him.

Chicken for dinner was very rare then but one Sunday we were going to have chicken for our lunch. At the same time Tom had disappeared from his house. My Sister and I put 2 and 2 together and made 4 – Tom was our lunch.

We said to Mum – 'I'm not eating Tom. She and Dad assured us that it was not Tom. What had happened was Frank next door wanted Tom as he didn't have a cockerel and in return he gave us a roasting chicken. Oh, I guess this is ok then.

My Sister and I enjoyed our chicken lunch.

I noticed both Mum and Dad did not eat their chicken – QED. As soon as you name an animal it is difficult to eat it.
I used to collect the eggs every morning and put them to one side and pick them up again on my way back home from school and put them in our egg bowl.

On two or three occasions I left the eggs in my pocket and took them to school – amazingly none were broken. It was obvious I was not going to be a businessman otherwise I would have sold them and told my Mum that the hens hadn't laid today.

I am now 9 and together with my Father we built a tree house in a relatively large pear tree. The floor was an old cellar door that used to be a way into a basement for barrels of beer at the local pub. This was held up by ropes, but I have no idea where these came from. My Uncle gave me a rope ladder which got me and my Sister (aged 5 or 6) up into it.

My Aunt lived in a hut in the grounds of a riding stable and my cousins used to work on the local farm during weekends and school holidays – sounds good – so my mother used to put me on a 144 bus with the fare telling the bus conductor to put me off at The Ivy Pub.

Wonderful days, I used to bring the cows in and feed the pigs.

I also used to ride Tom, the enormous Shire or Suffolk Punch horse who had to walk round and round in circles to drive an elevator to get sheaves of wheat and oats up to the top of the haystacks.

My Mother got paid for my work, being given 12 eggs when she and my Dad collected me in the evening with my Sister. We would then, if it was a Sunday, go to the local pub. My Sister and I would have lemonade outside and sometimes an arrowroot biscuit or bag of crisps. The game was to be the first to find the little blue bag of salt hiding in the crisps.

My father was forever in his shed making something. "I'm going to make a one string fiddle out of Uncle Wilf's cigar box that you can play". Interesting!

A 1" x 1" hole was made in the end of the box and a length of 1" x 1" wood was pushed into the hole and glued to the box lid. The lid was also glued down to make a sealed box.
"Frets" about 4" long x ½" wide were cut into the box lid, one each side of where the 1" x 1" wood was under the lid.

The wire, off of an old one – bar electric fire was unwound and stretched between the two wood screws. A very small hole was drilled through the screws to fix the wire ends. The screw at the far end could be turned to 'tune' the wire.

A cotton reel was jammed under the wire over the mid-part of the box.

I don't know where my Father got it but gave me a proper violin bow which when pulled over the wire made a musical note. The use of the word musical is doubtful.

Pressing the string down with my finger changed the note. He then moved on and built a dulcimer, but I won't bore you by describing its manufacturer. I think it had 17 strings which were whacked with drumsticks, fabulous. A few years later I made a double bass.

There were times on the farm in the summer when Ted, Frank, my cousin Robert, and me would sit on the fence by the pond under a willow tree and whittle.

We used to make whistles by whittling although Frank and Ted could make longer whistles with 2 or 3 holes along its length to enable 3 or 4 different notes to be played.

I was very pleased to make a simple whistle though under Ted's instruction.

Back then we all carried a knife which was used on the farm to cut bales open and endless other things including cutting a nice round piece of willow tree branch about 5/8" diameter and 6" long.

Sometimes we would give it a good beating all round to release the outer 'skin' from the central wood, but other times by rolling it in our palms the skin loosened and could be slipped off.

Just prior to slipping off a 'v' notch was cut 1/3 of the way through and the wedge-shaped piece removed.

After removing the inside wood, we would cut along the wood from the end and remove this piece – put the skin back on and you have a whistle.

I have to admit it was a little more complicated than this but well worth you having a go or better still get a good book on whittling.

Nowadays, the smell of cow dung always reminds me of whittling. Happy days.

I got interested in 2 areas, one was elephants and wildlife and two was electronics (or electrics as it was known then).

1952

I used to get on a 150 bus to a Government Surplus Shop in Manor Park where I would spend ages just staring at the wonderful array of things for sale, but having very little money could not buy much. This is the same shop as Lord Alan Sugar mentions in his book. I remember seeing the reels of films he bought in the window.

However, I did buy 2 sets of earphones and some wire. This enabled me, together with David next door, to talk to each other via a wire running over the roofs.

I loved elephants, having read every book in the Library about them.

You have all seen programmes on the TV about elephants so I won't bore you further, but you may not know, other than the great apes (including us), elephants are the only animal that has its boobs between its front legs. All others have their teats on their belly or between their back legs on an udder.

At about this time I was interested in various pets, I remember keeping grass snakes, a rat, mice, hamster, rabbits, and guinea pigs. I had a pet slow worm – this looks like a smooth brown snake but is actually a lizard without legs. I used to enjoy chasing my cousin Carol with what she thought was a dangerous snake – she hated it. The slow worm was equally stressed by Carol's screams. "Poor worm".

My Dad managed to convince my Mum that my sister no longer needed a pram and he and I would have it to make a soap box cart. A super-fast 2-seater was constructed with a brake and rope steering.

The King is dead.

School closes early and we all go home. Halfway home a letter box had been knocked over and smashed. A new one was fitted the next day with Queen Elizabeth II on it – the first in the country.

I was definitely a non-sporty type and dreaded the school sports day; however, everybody had to enter for at least one race or event.

Oh dear, I'm no good at anything. The teacher put me in the long jump and unbelievably I came 3rd. I think this was due to me running away from the Sports Master whenever I saw him.

We are now holidaying in a minute village called Wrabness in Essex on the River Stour in a caravan.

Water had to be pumped up from underground with a genuine picture book hand pump and aimed into our tank which has wheels fitted and a long-curved handle such that we could pull it. Fortunately, the farm was uphill to the pump, so we pulled it uphill empty and downhill when full.

I got to know a crow – I would feed him/her anything that I thought it would like. He/she would perch on my hand.

Interesting, when I returned the following year, he/she would come and find me. I could never get it to talk. In the field which housed our caravan lived a small black horse that I name Blacky. I used to climb on his/her back and get him/her going and steered by gently pulling his/her hair. His/her mane was quite long,

Lovely horse.

1953

I was hopeless at school much to the displeasure of my Father.
When I went 'up' to junior school from the infants I was put into Class '4R' – 'R' standing for retarded and most of the time I was sat at the back of the class tearing up newspaper to make papier mâché.

One day a visiting math's teacher took over our class who was teaching averages and fractions – I followed everything he said was shooting my hand up to answer his questions. He was contacted by my normal teacher asking why I was in 4R – I suddenly found myself in 3C and enjoyed lessons from then on especially math's.

Then the dreaded 11 plus exam – I failed miserably – but no worries this would send me to the Secondary School where they did metal and Woodwork! – Wonderful.

About this time my Dad took an interest in Budgerigars and had 8 breeding pairs, watching their behaviour was the total of my official sex education except for my Dad pointing to a mating pair asking if I knew what they were doing. Yes Dad – I wish I had asked him if I could answer any questions he had!

I had to go to the dentist, but I have no recollection why. At the age of 11, I was excessively skinny, I can't remember how much I weighed but I do know that I knew at the time and always added 1 stone on, pretending I was bigger than I was.

The dentist asked me what I weighed and of course I exaggerated by a stone – then that awful smell of rubber when the mask was held over my mouth and told to take some deep breaths.

The next thing I know is I am travelling down this dark tunnel towards a bright light at the end passing all the people I didn't like very much, including my Aunt Olive and Aunt Flory.

I had strong rubber bands tied to my legs and arms powerfully pulling me backwards, then wow, high speed backwards and somebody shouting 'Barry', 'Barry' 'Barry' at the top of their voices

I came round from the gas with 3 or 4 people round me. My Mother was sent for to take me home.

I lived next door, and the dentist was on the top floor above Bearstow Eaves the Estate Agent.

All vividly still recalled by my cousin Mary. Did I die?

You may be interested in hearing my view on what happens when you die.
If you are religiously minded you will have a clear idea of the answer, although having had some 10 years of religion instruction, Church of England biased, I don't remember being taught what happens at and after death but perhaps I didn't listen too well.

I did a short course on Buddhism, who believe you can start another life after death although in Tibet 29 days can exist between death and re-birth.

Buddhism is a wonderful way of life – I shall tell you more later when I visit Laos.

People who used to rely on religion for help, I believe now telephone the Council – I feel I may get into serious trouble for this, but it is my thought.

When you are busy time seems to go by quickly. When you are bored, or un-busy time goes by slowly.

So: very very busy = very very fast time   Very very un-busy = very very slow time.

You could plot a curve, busyness verses speed of time going past. If you are infinitely un-busy time will go by infinitely slow at the ultimate limit in that instant of death, time lasts forever! So – you do carry on after death, but only to you.

Uncle Wilf got a new car – it's a Zodiac and you won't believe it but it's pink.
Zodiac was launched by Ford in 1953 and with its 2.2 litre engine could do 84 mph and 0-60 mph in 20.4 seconds. Around town one got 20 mpg, but 23 mpg was advertised.

Wilf was only about 4' 9" high and the supplying garage bolted wooden blocks to the pedals such that he could reach them with the seat right forward.

I used to wash his car once or twice a month and he paid me 5 shillings a time – 25 pence today. Wilf's wife was Florence who I mentioned seeing at the dentist.

According to my Father, theatre land figured in the family history and was disappointed that I had no draw to the stage. Nevertheless, he joined me up with the Junior Magic Circle and I attended their meetings. I think fortnightly near Grants Hill just off of Wanstead Park Road – a short bus ride away.

My hands were too small to learn basic sleight of hand card moves and was told to go and buy a patient's pack (these are about 2/3 the size of a full pack.

I used to get the 144-bus home and would travel with an older guy – probably 16 or 17 years old.

One evening we sat in the back seat of the bus upstairs, and he got his cigarettes out – "would you like one"? – "yes please" I said, never even touched a cigarette previously. He used his lighter to light mine and the flame was some 4 or 5 inches high – I dodged away quickly but it singed my left eyebrow – I could smell the burning.

The second time all went ok – I was smoking!

On arriving home my Mother noticed my eyebrow – I explained exactly what happened. She opened her cigarettes (Players Weights) and said ok have one of mine I like to see a man smoke (a bit different today).

From then on I knew it was ok to smoke but in fact I didn't start seriously until I was 18.

When working on the farm and it was harvesting time I would sit on the binder. This was a machine towed by Frank on his tractor. The machine had large wooden slats fixed to spokes on an 8'-0" wheel that went round to stand the wheat up as it went along so it could be cut by the cutter under my feet. The lengths of straw carrying the wheat at one end was then cleverly bunched together and tied with string from a huge ball.

However, as the entire field had been sown with wheat seed, the tractor binder could not get into the field without ruining an area of crop. This was the only time I saw Mr. Smith, the owner of the farm. He would arrive with a huge picture book scythe and hand cut an area of wheat just inside the gate to enable the tractor and 'my' binder to make a start.

The wheat he cut had to be bundled up by hand tied with some of 'my' string. These tied bundles were called Sheaves.
The sheaths were then thrown (dropped) away from my machine and tractor, leaving them spread all over the field.

Sometimes the string would break, and I would shout to Frank to stop while I tied the ends together. Later that day or perhaps the next day we would do stooking. This entailed walking the field and standing 2 sheaths on end in a triangle, then 2 were placed next to them until we had a little house made (I think) 10 sheaves.

I would then add another one to each end, when it was then called a stook.

After the stooks were nice and dry (no moisture meters in those days) the stooks would be broken down into sheaves again and loaded onto a trailer and taken back to the farm.

I have just 'gone up' from the boy scouts cubs to scouts – the 4th Ilford troop.

This was a Scottish troop and once every, I think, month we marched around the roads on a Sunday behind a bagpipe and drum band.

I wanted to learn the pipes, but my parents did not have the money to purchase a set of pipes for me. I was awarded with lots of badges for learning various crafts.

1955

I could find no interest at school in Geography, History, Holy Scripture, or P.T.

What jobs, when I leave school require an in-depth knowledge of these subjects to make money other than teaching them?

"Please Sir, may I do metalwork instead of history?" was often being spoken by me and perhaps 30% of lessons I was allowed to switch – I was going to be an Engineer and that was final.

Jumping ahead I am now (until I retired) a Fellow of the Chartered Institute of Building Services Engineers specialising in Renewable Energy and Air Conditioning.

In 2019, there were only 1095 of us Fellows worldwide. I don't know how many there are in Britain. We are a rare lot.

I have to admit; I do wish I had listened to Mr. Spicer and his History and Geography as later on I would travel the world delivering engineering.

By now if a pupil was very naughty at school there was always the cane and book – the headmaster had to approve caning and sign in a 'caning book' the reason for the punishment.
I was never caned but it did look painful – 'hold your hand out, palm up'! A lesser punishment was a slipper (plimsoll), 'bend over pose'. You ended up with a sore bum.

Well, what did we do for amusement during good weather? One thing was to walk to Valantines Park Lake with Brian and pay for 1 hour's use of Skiffs.

These are single-seater rowing boats with a sliding seat, so by pushing your feet against 'stops' one could put a lot of power into a stroke. The guy managing the facility would sometimes recommend we wait for (say) number 17 to come in as it had a better mechanism. He knew we were quite good.

As the boats are very narrow the rowlocks for the oars to rest in stick out the side by some 2.5 ft. You had to have a good sense of balance to get into the narrow boat but once in, there was a clockwise routing plan especially for the young guys taking their girlfriends for a vintage 'sail' with the young lady sitting in the quite wide seat at the back with ropes from the rudder fed over her shoulders such that she could steer. Quite good really, to turn to the left, pull the left rope and vice versa. There was no reverse gear!

As everybody generally sailed round the edge of the lake the centre was left fairly clear. The central 'lane' of course, has no preferred direction. This is out patch.

We could go from end to end at high speed with nobody getting in our way. It felt like we were doing 50 mph.
On other occasions, after school – school finished at 5 past 4 Brian, and I would walk down to the pitch and putt facility. There, the facility manager would hire us a No. 7 iron and a putter and one golf ball. We got quite good and looking back I am surprised neither of us took up golf as an adult hobby.

I need a hobby – foreign birds sound interesting so let's build an aviary. In the 1950's foreign finches and other smaller birds were imported in their thousands and could be obtained quite cheaply.

I purchased weaver birds – these built interesting nests.

I soon had a pair (boy and girl) of Napoleon Weavers (they are yellow birds), Orange Weavers (which are of course orange) and four Red Billed Weavers (who are grey with a red beak). I also had Java Sparrows and Cut Throat Finches.

Later on, I moved to British birds with Bull Finches.

1956

About this time word had it that a new sound system was going to arrive called stereophonic and a few "stereo" records were available. A friend of mines Father was involved in the development of the special stereophonic cartridges that fitted on the end of the record player arm. These had 4 pins on the back, such that 2 could be connected to a left-hand amplifier and loudspeaker, and the other two to the right. My friend was lucky enough to obtain a rejected cartridge and a second one came along for me!

Wow, this is exciting; stuff, by connecting to a radio set on one side and my tape recorder the other, a demonstration record issued by Decca caused steam trains to pass through the room. Unbelievable!

It wasn't long before we were building huge loudspeaker cabinets, some 4 feet high to give full frequency stereophonic sound, these would deliver unbelievable bass down to about 40 cycles per second (Hertz now).

About this time, I had my first sexual experience with a young girl who helped looking after the horses at my Aunt's place. I was thrilled with her wanting a quick grope, and each weekend we got more daring but never actually had sex – I guess if we had I might have to sack myself.

It was all very satisfying.

After her (and my) fun I would walk down the hill to the Farm where I worked in the afternoons. My normal job would be to get the cows in. Fortunately, they all knew the way so all I had to do was to get behind them and shout, 'go on' and clap my hands. One time, however, a cow had calved, and she would not move whatever I did. I ran back to the farm and told Frank. He said – get on the tractor and we will drive down to her. On arrival with great courage (I thought) we picked up the calf and laid it on the trailer – he drove slowly back to the farm and the cow followed – I went last to keep the cow going. All ended well. The calf was a boy so I asked Frank if we could call it Barry or Winston. He agreed it could be Winston. I was dead chuffed!

I used to be able to climb in the top half of the Bull's door which was normally open and stupidly (looking back) sit on his back, he liked his neck scratched. I did this quite often without a problem but one late afternoon my Mum and Dad turned up to collect me – I normally walked up the hill to the pub where they parked their Austin Seven car, but they came to the farm. I said – watch this.

As I climbed on Tom's back he jumped round I fell off. My Mum screamed, which brought Frank over to us who let the bull out while I got down by his trough and where Tom wasn't, I picked myself up. We then had to catch him – not easy and I and my Mum and Dad were ordered (in a friendly voice) away from the yard – in fact we went into the Dairy where my Mum always likes to chat to Mrs. Smith whilst she was cooling the milk.

1957

Age 15, time to leave school unless I could stay on for another year such that I could take the GCE exams and actually get certificates!

Parties were the thing, and our age group were buying record players and turning the volume up at parties.

"Oh dear", no good us buying one as both Brian's and my home were fed with D.C. (Direct Current) electricity which would not operate the new record players.

"No problem", generate our own. We acquired a unit that consisted of a DC motor driving an AC generator – called an alternator. This thing had to be watched as halfway through a party it would overheat and we didn't want it to catch fire as that would have paused the dancing – including jiving which had just arrived from America. Friends would arrive with their 45 rpm records threaded on a cord through the central hole and dangle them going to and from parties.

My first 45 rpm was "Only Sixteen" by Tommy Steel. At the same time my Dad was buying some old cheap electric workshop equipment for his shed as he knew that we were soon going to be switched to the new AC electricity and the Government would replace all DC driven equipment with new!

1958

We are getting quite good at wood and metalwork at school, both Brian and I made oscillating steam engines in metalwork and trays and bookcases in woodwork – these were going to be submitted as part of our GCE examinations.

Unbelievably the corners of the bookcases had to be made with 'secret mitred dovetail joints.

I couldn't work out why the dovetails – damn difficult to make – had to be there if nobody saw them behind the mitred corners. Fortunately, the examiner believed they were there. Brian's was super quality and I helped him carry it home. Don't know what happened to mine.

The woodwork and metalwork teacher was Mr. Write. Looking back, it was his love of his subjects that rubbed off on us.

We both became Engineers, Brian rising to the ultimate top. I went to a Publics Work Congress later in 1974 and surprise surprise Brian was speaking.

We finish school in July or August, and it is planned to 'put on' a show which parents and friends will pay to come and see.

I was to be the door mouse at the Mad Hatters Tea Party in Wind in the Willows. I was surprised the Headmaster would allow such a horror play in the school – for example I had my head jammed into a tea pot at the Mad Hatter's Tea Party. It is interesting to note that the Mad Hatter left the price tag on his top hat showing he paid 10/6 (ten shillings and six pence (55 pence now).

Brian and I were to wire all the stage lighting (health and safety and wiring regulations were not yet invented).
Believe it or not my Father taught me to test if a wire was live by brushing your finger very quickly across the bare wire end – if you didn't get a shock the power was probably turned off!

So, I knew what a shock felt like.

I went home at 5 to 4 one evening having half wired a light. Picked up my tools the next day and got a shock from the wire that was dead yesterday.

The Headmaster made an announcement at assembly the following morning "anybody found on the stage without authority will be caned".

The stage was quite empty from this time on.

For some reason I cannot remember, two cannons had to be fired near the end of the show.

Mr. Hoars, the Science Master came up with a plan for the bang, fire a starting pistol into a metal waste bin – surprisingly it sounded quite loud.

For the flash, a small plate with a measured amount of flash powder on it and to make it flash, a spark from a 12-volt car battery did the trick.

Brian flashed and I banged on being given a cue. I think the play was performed on 3 nights. Well, the 3rd performance was on the last day of school for all the pupils except a few, so never mind about the carefully measured amount of flash powder let's put a couple of scoops on the plate!

BANG/FLASH.

The school hall was filled with smoke and many Mums and Dads were coughing!

Some white powder seemed to only land on dark blue men's suits! We were told off but with a big grin on the teacher's face. What Fun.
Took GCE exams and managed to pass Metal Work, Woodwork, General Science and Engineering Drawing.

Walking across the playground, the duty teacher called me over saying – 'Pitt, have you got a job yet? – No Sir – well go to this interview Wednesday – thank you Sir.

I was told to take with me a model steam engine I had made but I didn't know why.

I got home to tell my Father that I had got the job even though I didn't know what they did.

However – my Father knew the firm and explained to me that they were heating engineers and indeed my Father had worked with the company.

I started as an Apprentice in September 1958 being paid Two Pounds, Fourteen Shillings, and Seven Pence per week, of which I gave my Mother One Pound leaving me with £1.70 in new money.

I am offered a motor bike quite cheap, £7-00 I think. It was a very dirty Francis Barnett. I took it completely apart and repainted it dark red.
Put it all together and rode it down the garden path just down to the Aviary where a glossy starling had escaped. He had cost me £2-00 – saved up from Christmas and birthday gifts.

Fortunately, now I had a Francis Barnet motorbike I could get to work – some 12 miles away.

The motor bike was I think a 1929 model which I had previously taken apart and re-painted.

I was forever stopped by the Police for not having a speedometer – I learned the 1934 (I think) Road Traffic Act that said if registered before 1934 no speedometer was necessary. To get into first gear with my hand gear change lever situated on the side of the petrol tank to get going I had to walk along until the gears lined up.

1959

I acquired a very unusual 'Southbend Lathe" Wow – what can I make. I spent many years making odds and ends – also spending time re-building my Francis Barnet motorbike.

1960

I took Veronica out for a drink; I think this was my second date with her and the first time for a sit-down evening meal. I have a terrible habit of calling all girls I like 'Pet' – I know they don't like it but I still do it.

The conversation went like this - 'you're going to have chicken I believe – so would you like white wine'? Oooh I love white wine, when I hold the glass I am mesmerised by the colour and the little bubbles dancing in the glass. The aroma is scintillating and when the nectar flows over my tongue I hear choirs of heavenly angels singing the most beautiful choruses – on the other hand, red wine makes me fart.

So, we had some red wine – I think Nui St George.

As part of my apprenticeship, I had to work on site as a fitter's mate.
This sometimes included making the tea for Bill and Frank, sometimes others if somebody had turned up such as a lorry driver.
The method of tea making was simple, but I now know could be dangerous – so you must not do this – stick to the electric kettle or a gas hob.

On site for a new school in Romford, facilities were very limited – I remember the consultant who designed the heating system we were installing was Miss Nobbs – she must have been a capable engineer as we were installing a differential steam system.

Unusual to say the least! However, to make the tea you set two bricks on edge close to oxygen and acetylene welding equipment which hopefully somebody had left close our chairs.

We always kept one galvanised bucket clean for our tea. This bucket had 4 mugs full of water tipped in if I was making tea for 3 people and 3 spoons of tea stirred in.
I'm not going to tell you how to light the oxygen/acetylene 'torch' as although not exactly dangerous could back-fire with an enormous bang throwing you away from the bucket.

When you had a clear flame just a touch of yellow maybe – we don't want a flame of 1000° Centigrade on our bucket, nor too yellow which would cause our nice clean bucket to go black – it was a very exacting time of day.

Place the torch under the bucket and in 9 or 10 minutes there was tea for all. The conversation at 'teatime' was sometimes interesting. Word had it that the guy hodding over there (pointing) may become a famous singer as he had been offered an important contract – later I learned they were talking about Tom Jones.

It was on this site that a helicopter arrived to take an injured guy to hospital – I have told you about this elsewhere.

Later, on this contract, the 'Laggers' (those who applied insulation to the pipework) had started mixing their powdered asbestos with something else and water, then plastered it onto the pipework. After setting, the final coat of plaster was beautifully finished and then painted.

The mixing was done in an old fashioned 'tin-bath' (actually galvanised) and the air in the room was filled with asbestos powder which we were all breathing even though it caused us to cough.

 We now know this damages our lungs.

Now, at the time of writing, in 2022/2023 my breathing is difficult and in 2016 it was confirmed by way of my 'patient discharge summary':

"Right lung partial collapse – right pleural basal thickening due to previous asbestos exposure".

I am not sick enough for compensation!

Beginning to take a <u>very minor</u> interest in classical music. Three of us went off to the Albert Hall on the suggestion of Brian.

The cheapest seats were not seats, but if you took sufficient newspaper you could climb a million stairs and lay on them right up the top! We thought we were promenading but I still don't know if that extends to upstairs!

We heard Tchaikovsky 1812 – they had real cannons and fired them at the end – absolute opposite to how Dane School taught music – playing the most boring stuff possible putting us all off for life – how stupid! We even had to sit on the floor in the hall and listen to a quartet – terrible.

A quartet should consist of – I have since found out of 2 violins, 1 viola and 1 cello. I don't remember them having a cello – so they couldn't even get that right!

Whilst thinking about Junior School us boys were housed downstairs and the girls upstairs.

The Headmaster came into our room and said the school was arranging dancing classes for our age group, DANCING CLASSES! Whatever next. Upstairs we went – form two lines, one of boys and opposite one of girls. The person opposite you would be your partner for the following lesson.

The 2 girls roughly opposite me both went to the 2 guys on each side of me – the one that lost got me.

I found out later her name was Annette. I liked her!

The lesson was the dance called the Valita – of no use at all I've never been to a dance and required this knowledge.

Just as bad as the music lessons – best stick to metalwork and math's, that's what I thought.

The only thing I actually remember from this lesson is you had to start with your feet turned out – but they never said how many degrees – not many people can do more than 15° without falling over – you try.

If you want to try the Valita your best bet is to get 2 drums tuned to F and C and hit them in this order (I think FC FC FC FC – and dance to that)
An even better idea is to pay for professional lessons.

1961

Brian's Mother thought us boys should learn to dance, and we joined up for lessons in Barkingside – Roy Lance Studios. When we turned up there were normally enough girls such that we all had partners to learn with.
One week I met a rather attractive girl also called Annette and suggested we dance together the next week, and I would wait outside for her. Next week arrived and I waited until it was past the start time – I was about to go in when another young lady arrived at the door at the same time – I said "shall we go in together, she said ok. Her name was Yvonne, and we were married 7 years later.

In the beginning I just saw her to the bus stop. After 4 or 5 weeks, my firm, S J Frith & Son had a job come in to install new toilets in the playground at Yvonne's school – I went to see the boss and asked if I could manage this job myself – he agreed. For untrue reasons. I had to visit site every 2 or 3 days and it was strange that the meetings were always when break time occurred, even so we never met though at the school!

One night I saw her home and she suggested I went in with her to meet her Mum and Dad. Wow, on entry her Grandma was reading teacups! – She was a fortune teller. Well, I, being interested in Engineering & Science did not believe in such rubbish. However, I pretended I did and asked if she could read my fortune.

A quick cup of tea was made which I had to drink.

Now it was obvious that she knew nothing about me whatsoever. She started: -

"Your friend with a small blue car is going abroad very soon – a long way to the left –probably America."

My friend Peter had a blue car but he's not going abroad – in fact he's just got a new job in this Country.

"There is an old lady in your family perhaps your Grandma" (good guess?) "Who has a broken hip and is in great pain" – no that is not right – yes it is!

Had to be very careful on my motor bike, I can see a broken leg.

I went home. I could see my Mother on the phone in the house though the reeded glass door, on entering with my key. My Mother said this is Barry now – I'll get him to bring me over in his Father's car.

Unbelievable – Grandma – called Nana had just fallen downstairs and the ambulance was there.

The next day we were told she had broken her hip. Even more unbelievable, the day after Peter came round to tell me his new Company was seconding him to America!

I'm off to the National College to obtain a diploma in Environmental Engineering. This is high level heat transfer right up to complex air conditioning I was due to start close to Borough Station on September 4th.

Unfortunately, I was hit by a hit and run driver and came off my motorbike – I was just sitting on it at the roadside when a green sports car swerved into me on 30th August.

It took some time to repair my bike, but at least I wasn't hurt other than a cut leg. In 2 days, my left leg was very swollen from the knee down. Off I went to Hospital for an x-ray on the orders of my GP Doctor who I saw in the first place.

I had damaged an artery and I was instructed to lie down for 2 weeks with my left leg held well above my head if we had added some bandages and a hook in the ceiling. I would make a good cartoon! In fact, I had to miss 3 weeks of college and I found it difficult to catch up as all disciplines had started with basic principles.

Fortunately, some matters I already used at work.

The doctor, after 1 week, came to see my leg – he said you could have trouble with this leg later in life.

Later, you will see I nearly lost this leg in 2014. My brilliant surgeon did not appear interested in what happened 50 years ago. I still believe there is/was a connection.

A couple of times during these 50 years a small chip of glass would pop out of my leg at the wound area!

Nevertheless, I passed, and received my Diploma.

We were 17 and looked old enough to drink pints of beer and the four lads all had motorbikes and scooters.
So, off to the Beehive Pub every Friday night where Wally would play the organ and choose songs that we could sing.

A favourite was "I'm Henry the Eighth I am" and we found that once we got going most of the pub would join in.

You may be interested in the words:

I'm Henry the eighth I am Henry the eighth I am, I am
I got married to the widow next door,
She's been married seven times before,
And everyone was a Henry,
She wouldn't have a Willy or a Sam I'm her eighth old man,
I'm Henry Henry the eighth.

You will obviously want to know that it began life in 1910 as a Music Hall number by Fred Murray and R. P. Weston.

EMI released a recording in September 1965 with the word Willy changed to William – I wonder why?

During Bank Holiday weekends a group of us would head off to Durdle Door and Lulworth Cove.

Peter would normally take with him a telephone and length of cable. Having got down a punishing zig zag path to the beach, the blankets and towels were laid out as our base camp.

Peter would then place his old-fashioned telephone close to the water's edge and bury the wire all the way up to our base area from where he could make it ring and talk to anybody who may be tempted to answer it.

An interesting physiological experiment took place. When adults heard it ringing, they would make a diversion up the beach to keep as far away from the telephone as possible.

When Mum & Dad went past with a child they would normally suggest to the child to answer it, which they normally did.

Peter "have you been a good boy/girl" – "yes". "Well, this is Father Christmas, and I will give you a tick in my book – bye bye – have a lovely day"

The kids usually looked quite excited. Just along from our base Peter would have buried a manikin's leg leaving the calf and foot sticking out of the sand. He always put a longish sock on the leg, so the dummy look was hidden.

Virtually everybody avoided it!

1964

My 3 friends creating the '4 lads' decided to go fishing on the first day of the season (there is a period when fishing is not permitted allowing the fish to breed.

In the meantime, we decided to hire a small boat on a huge lake in the Norfolk Broads.

Unfortunately, the lake (more like a sea) was quite rough and as we got out into the centre of the lake one of my friends felt quite seasick and indeed was actually sick losing his false tooth overboard. He was not happy and fortunately fell asleep.

One of the other guys had a false tooth and I suggested I borrow his 'plate' and I'll tie it on to my fishing line and pretend to catch his tooth when he woke up. Oh dear! He woke and I said wow look what I have caught – I gave them to him, and he said No, they are not mine and threw them overboard! Now two of us had no teeth! I felt very guilty!

I decided to grow a beard – it did look rather tatty. Coming out of Ilford Station one evening a Policeman approached me and asked (told?) me to stand in an identification parade. I agreed and ended up standing in line with some of the ugliest guys in Ilford. A young girl walked up and down, and I was terrified she would choose me. She didn't – I went home and shaved my so-called beard off – Never again.

The 4 lads decided to go to Rome for a week plus 1 week driving there with stops and one week back.

I think we were going to drive through 7 countries, so we needed some cash in each of these countries for petrol and snacks. If we stopped we could always change some British Pounds – which we were taking.

We were virtually out of petrol in Germany one night – no problem we had German cash. Wow, having filled the car the cashier said our money was no good. Apparently we had the new Mark notes that he had not seen before. Fortunately, he was able to telephone somebody and described the note.

Finally, he accepted them.

Driving about 11.00 p.m. through the black forest, miles from anywhere we heard music coming from the hills to our right.

We turned right at the next junction to investigate – the road went on and on for perhaps 5 miles when we came across a clearing with loud music and dancing.
We parked and several Germans came over to us – was this ok?

We were made very welcome. Fortunately, one of us agreed not to drink the vast amounts of beer we were offered – he drove, neat.

On the way to Rome, we stopped on the Adriatic coast in Italy (right hand one) at Pescara and spent most of the first day sleeping on the beach having done a big drive the day and night before. We were given a hooter entering the beach close to a kiosk (squeezy type). If we wanted anything, blow the hooter and a lad would come running to take our order – good idea as the beach was very wide and a long way to the sea.
We were the only 4 guys on the beach as far as the eye could see.
We then took the main road which goes straight across to Rome.

Empty road, poodling along, perhaps 80 mph, all of a sudden 'BANG', halfway across an old car pulled out of a side road and we were hit by it.

We hid all our money save about £5.00 in secret places in the car that we had pre-planned. Our car was drivable, but we don't want Italian police chasing us across Italy.
Very soon 7 or 8 villagers were surrounding us and then the Priest arrived to bless the accident. You must pay – no you should not pull out of a side road without stopping or looking NO YOU MUST PAY. I forget how many Lira (about £20.00 then) – This lady is hurt – no she wasn't here when the collision occurred anyway – it's a pimple.

We better do what they say – we follow them to the local doctor. Treatment will be Lira (£7.00).

We all turned out our pockets and had about £6.00 between us – we gave them all our money pulling our pocket linings out to prove we had no more and gave it to them – OK YOU GO!

All good for the book!

On pitching camp in Rome people asked where we got our suntan – England we would say – the Romans did not believe us.

We noticed that the local population dressed similar to us and not in Togo's and leather skirts for the men – all our books at school were clearly wrong.

The Romans looked nothing like Mr. Spicer said they would look like, no leather skirts, shields, or swords – I always thought he wasn't too sure of his geography.

Back then not many Romans spoke English – but on Rome's beaches with about 8 of us there was an English/German speaker, a German/French, and a French/Italian.

The only common language was chemical. We all knew H_2O, H_2SO_4 and a few others.

The woman among us wanted to see English money and showed her a 10-shilling note – ARRR – BELLA BELLA QUEENI. Roughly meaning lovely, lovely Queen. We found out that Romans loved our Queen. This probably stems from the time the Romans left us some 2018 years and 3 months ago. We were leaving to go to the Colosseum tomorrow, so via 3 translators we asked one of the Roman guys what it was like – Don't know never been there. What! We have come 3,000 miles to see it. He wanted to know if we had seen Westminster Abbey. 2 of us said NO!

We drove home stopping at Paris. We were virtually out of money now and back then there were no credit or debit cards and getting money even if you had some was a major dilemma. Do I go up the Eiffel Tower in Paris or do I buy my then girlfriend Yvonne a present?

I went up the Eifel Tower but didn't like it so wished I had bought her a scarf with a picture of the Eifel Tower on it!

Having now got an interest in becoming an engineer after school, I thought I should study mathematics. A good start would be to better my mental arithmetic and to assist this I trained my brain to deal with short cuts.

These are the easiest ones to remember:

To multiply a 2-digit number by 11 simply write down the number, add the two figures and put the answer in the middle, e.g., 27 x11 = 297 (9 = 2+7)

To multiply by 9, add a 0 to the number and then subtract the number.

e.g., 31 x 9 = 310 – 31 = 279

To check if your 9 x answers are correct the answers for lower figures will add up to 9 e.g., 7 x 9 = 63 (6 + 3 = 9), 13 x 9 = 117 (1 + 1 + 7 = 9)

I won't bore you further!

Took an interest in electric organs and collected old pianos to salvage the keyboards.

We only had valves then to generate the notes, but another way relied on little neon bulbs, these switch on at (I think) 90 volts and switch off at 70 volts. As the voltage decays the wave form was (is) a saw tooth wave by using capacitors and coils various tones can be obtained.

My Father managed to get me 100 of these lamps very cheap.

I made little circuit boards by etching the circuit I wanted on copper plated plastic and then etched away the copper I didn't want with Ferric Chloride.

I built a nice case, and the organ could be played.

I was given an oscilloscope which lets you see the wave forms of any tone.

I met a guy who played the trumpet and got him to come round and play a few notes. I copied the wave form from my oscilloscope but although I thought I was good at math's, I could not calculate the circuits necessary to convert my new trumpet sound from my saw tooth shape. My sister helped in winding coils as they were required.

Transistors were just arriving but expensive as the prices fell I was able to build a far better sounding organ using bare OC72 transistors.

In all my organs the keys pushed down on gold wires. I paid £1-8s-4p for 60 feet of 20-gauge gold wire!

My organ could provide the following 'voices':

Pedals

Bourdon	16 foot
Dulciona	16 foot
Violone	16 foot
Bass Flute	8 foot

Swell Keyboard (top one)

Tibia	16 foot
Flute	8 foot
Stopped flute	8 foot
Piccolo	2 foot
Violone	8 foot
Dulciona	8 foot
Salicet	4 foot
Kinvra	16 foot
Clarinet	8 foot
French Horn	8 foot
Cornopean	8 foot
Clarion	4 foot

Great Keyboard (lower one)

Bourdon	16 foot
Flute	8 foot
Melodia	8 foot
Flute	4 foot
Diapason	8 foot
Gamba	8 foot
Gemshorn	4 foot
Fifteenth	2 foot

3 or 4 of them sounded something like they should.

Today, the various sounds of the organ are digitally synchronised but back in my days there were no digit things other than fingers.

Some readers may be interested to know that if you take a saw tooth wave form and place a 1 Henry choke and a 0.064 uF capacitor to earth you convert the saw tooth to something like a French horn, or with a 0.02 uF capacitor something like a clarinet but feeding the saw tooth signal via a 0.1 uF capacitor to this tuned circuit.

A flute requires a choke of 10 Henry's and a capacitor of 390 pF in series with the signal as well as 2 x 0.00016 uF to each, and so it goes on. Many weeks were spent fiddling with the component values to get the right sounds – some were quite good.

I really must thank my sister Lesley for winding the chokes.

I purchased Mullard Type LA2 Ferroxcube cores and Lesley wound 1,640 turns of this copper wire (actually 45 swg 0.003 mm dia.) to give me 10 Henries or 5,200 turns of 48 swg wire for 15 Henries.

The thought of her losing count was very concerning, she never did! For the whole organ I needed 12. She was a good winder!

1965

Let's go to Cornwall. We four lads set out with camping gear and visited every cove and beach in Cornwall. I had a windscreen on my tiger cub motorbike and purchased a plastic triangular sticker at each stop. Soon the windscreen was full but no problem as I looked over it when driving.

I am beginning to be offered other jobs and joined a firm of consultants who seemed to specialise in tower blocks of flats and air force bases.
So, I am now working as a Consulting Engineer for H A Sandford & Partners working on an enormous 20 (I think) storey tower block.

Our Senior Partner, Mr. Parker, is going out to lunch with somebody and unbelievably asked me to go with him. We met a guy under the clock at Waterloo Station and we took a taxi to the Wig & Pen Club – wow this is big stuff to me. The two guys had a fascinating conversation "I hear you are a Freemason" – "No, are you", "No, I'm a Liveryman, "arh so am I."

The more they spoke the more I was determined to join their 'executive club' one day.

I said to Mr. Parker – is there some way I could join the Wig & Pen club? He pointed out that the last time he looked there was a 6 month's waiting list and you were interviewed.

In a couple of months' time, he asked if I would like to join him again, "YES PLEASE SIR", fine, it's Friday for lunch. On arrival Mr. Parker asked for 'his' form, told me to sign it. On handing it back to him he said – you are now a member. I felt 18 feet tall – I've joined the club!

After 25 years of membership, you are (were) permitted to wear a pink tie with the Wig & Pen Club insignia embroidered in black – I have one! During the 25 years I became well known, a major advantage in being a member, one could pop in for a drink during the times the pubs had to shut as required by Law.

If I took somebody to lunch who was itching to join – I used to do a Parker and get it arranged there and then. Even then the waiting list was several months. A story goes that a senior member invited a colleague to join him at the Wig & Pen Club. His colleague was late but finally telephoned to say he was in Wigan but couldn't find the Pen Club!
The Club was called 'Wig & Pen' as, for hundreds of years, being opposite the High Court it was where the Barristers (in wigs) met the journalists (with pens) and news was exchanged. The Club had two staircases serving 3 floors; both of these were the only staircases that survived the Great Fire of London for 4 days (2nd to 6th September 1666). Earlier finds in the basement indicated a history back to 1500!

I am informed (possibly quite wrongly) that the fire precautions were inadequate, and the club was made to close.

If true, more rubbish issued by Parliament, not allowing special cases.

I recall two interesting projects, one was a phone call from a Mr. Jack Coen, who wanted his office air conditioned (it was a hot July). I went to see him and discovered he owned Tesco's. When I gave him an idea of cost he thought it would be a better idea to fit 2 fans that could blow air into his office or blow it out from a button on his desk. He would not tell me what YCMMSOYA embroidered onto his tie stood for (see Appendix).

The Senior Partner, who wore a monocle, owned a wonderful, thatched cottage close to the south coast and in fantastic countryside. I was told that staff could borrow this at a very reasonable cost (I think it was £15.00 per week). Well, - worth a week or so.

I hired it for 1 week.

We arrived to find a staircase to upstairs and just half doors to the bedrooms.
The local pub was just a short walk away so off we went. The Locals wanted to know who we were and where we were staying and said in that case then you must know Frank Foster – Well yes, he was our Chief Draughtsman.

Apparently, Frank wanted to fart and was aware because of the half doors, everybody would hear. He noticed that the deep windowsill was level with the bed. Brilliant, he could get his bottom onto the sill; pull the curtain around him such that any noises went outside.

After the louder than normal fart, a voice from outside came back oh – I bet you enjoyed that then – it was the milkman who had arrived very early. The story is now well known around the village.

We could walk to the bakers where there would be a 20-minute wait if there was a queue of more than two or three whilst the scandal and rumours of the village were related and discussed, but well worth it to get their lardy cake – I guess this must have been several thousand calories but exquisite – we could always get freshly baked bread of course.

I was with H A Sandford & Partners, Mechanical and Electrical Consulting Engineers.

We were working on several housing sites that included Tower Blocks. We were instructed to design the heating and hot and cold-water services such that they will never break down (the leases and rental contracts stated that no money is payable if these services are not available).

This would normally mean that each flat should have its own system such that a breakdown would be restricted to that flat. However, the Council had passed a motion that larger sites should be provided with centralised services.

Answer – 3 pipes to a point close to each flat (mostly hidden - underneath access staircases). From there, just 2 pipes to serve both heating and hot water. Both pipes were connected directly to the hot water cylinder but connected via a non-return valve to the heating. Back in the boiler house, 1st week in April the flow and return pipes are reversed such that the flow cannot pass the non-return valve and the heating won't work during the summer. In September the pipes are reversed again to enable the heating to work.

3 pipes went from the boiler house to the various blocks of flats. Should there be a leak or problem, the spare pipe could be brought into service by manipulating 3-way valves.

It is interesting to note that Tower Blocks (up to 22 storeys) sink into the ground. In one case the figures we were given were 2" (50mm) during building a further 30mm during the first 5 years. All incoming pipes had to be fitted with articulated levelling joints to allow this movement. Pipe slopes to enable air to be vented also had to be carefully considered.

1966

My Father has pains in his left leg and after a few months his toes went black with gangrene and his leg was amputated shortly after. His one complaint was that when he queued up at Roehampton Hospital for his false leg (prosthesis today) and when Group Captain Douglas Bader walked in he was shown to the front of the queue – not fair. Apparently we found later that Douglas Bader was a difficult person to get on with as I found out reading his book "Reach for the Sky".

I was asked if I would like to join a syndicate to own a caravan in France. Well, why not, I think the input was £100.00.

In a couple of years', it was my (our) turn to use the caravan. Off we went.

Zero excitement on arrival, it was one of the smallest caravans I have seen and rocked when the wind blew. Not only that, but the van was also situated on the edge of a raised area and in my opinion dangerous to say the least. The weather was dim and raining.
Don't like it – let's drive to Spain.
On the road to Spain the sky looked sunny right over the France/Spain border. We booked into a hotel close to the beach. Next day we sat on the beach amongst many others – I recognised a voice close to us incredibly! Wow, our neighbours worked at Jefferies as a senior supervisor where I worked.

Unbelievable.
On the way back to England we called in at a famous village in Pamplona, I think called San Fermin. It was now July, and we were puzzled as to why the streets were empty, but the pavements full! We were shouted at in Spanish but when somebody shouted in English "get over the fence" – well we never vaulted a fence so quick, just as we landed the other side 3 bulls came charging down the road.

This was a rehearsal for the world-famous San Fermin Bull Run which would be staged tomorrow.

All the signs were in Spanish – not sure why!

1967

Having got married in 1967 we moved into a new house in Lodge Lane, Romford, Essex knowing a telephone would not be available for several months and could be a year.

At this time the BT Tower was being constructed. It was decided to incorporate a "chairman's flat' within the building at the base of the Tower in Howland Street such that the chair or other important persons could stay in London at the late meetings and this flat will be built to latest thoughts including the very latest silent air conditioning.

I was asked if I could provide such a system. Of course, I said yes.

Everybody was pleased with the results. The only thing outstanding was the preparation of maintenance documentation.

The chairman was planning to stay there shortly and requested the telephone number of the installer in case anything went wrong as his own service engineers had no instructions.

The only person who knew how it all worked was me and I had no phone.

We were one of the last to move into our Estate and about 1 mile from the nearest telephone service.
At six thirty Sunday morning there is a banging on the door. Outside was a truck with several telephone poles on board and several other telephone vans.

By late evening we were on the phone!

Wow, big trouble, virtually a total of 150 other houses rioted – why does last one in be the only one with a telephone.

I had to contact BT at Director Level to convince them to install phones to the other 149 houses; they were all on the phone within a week.

The chairman did not have to phone me.

About this time a friend gave us a turkey – although dead still had his (her?) feathers on. I had to pluck it and removed his (her?) internal organs.

Although I wore an apron I seemed to get covered in blood. Just then the doorbell sounded – carrying my carving knife and covered in blood I opened the door. My neighbour shouted WHERES YVONNE!! Oh dear – I didn't think.

Although we moved in in 1967 the fences separating the back gardens had not been completed and there was a missing first section enabling our neighbour to visit us via the back garden, and us visit him (or her!).

We had a small dog and next door had a rabbit which lived in a hutch. One afternoon we found our dog with next doors rabbit in its mouth – obviously having killed it.

Oh dear. The guy next door will go berserk. I had an idea, I got the rabbit off of the dog it was filthy, obviously been dragged through the mud. I washed it and then dried it with our hairdryer and then after dusk placed it back in its hutch – next door will think his rabbit died through natural causes in its hutch. The next morning, we were very nervous, the guy next door was coming up our path. I opened the door when he knocked. 'GUESS WHAT' he said.

Yesterday my rabbit died, I buried it and now IT'S BACK IN ITS HUTCH! I suggested a cup of tea.
1970

Our first son is born, resulting in me having to buy an expensive 'Silver Cross' pram and all the accessories. I chose one with suitable wheels to make a good go-cart.

My wife was in hospital for 2 days when the Registrar turned up to register the baby. We could not agree on his middle name.

Initially my wife wanted Paul as his first name generating Pulpit as his popular name – no good, so Antony was chosen. His middle name was to be chosen from Arthur, Charles, William, or Winston. She decided to give them all to him!

I decided to paint a picture of superman on his bedroom wall life size, but I'm not sure he appreciated it until he was 6 months old.

I'm working in Holborn, London, back then Holborn Tube Station was the deepest in the Country. It was a long way up to the top.

My office was on the 1st floor in Gate Street, which is a narrow walkway with a telephone box just outside our window.

One of the guys would phone the box just as (normally a young lady) was just going in to make a phone call – there were no mobiles then. With luck she would pick up the phone when it rang.

"Thank you for answering – this is the telephone engineer – have you got 2 minutes to help me check this telephone". "Yes", "ok thanks. I'm going to count to ten – please hold the phone 6" from your ear – one – two – ten, can you hear me", "Yes". "Thank you, could you please open the door, hold the phone about 2'-6" from your ear and count as loud as you can, one to ten".

He then opened the window and thanked her. He also glued a two-shilling piece to the pavement to watch a few people try and pick it up. Interestingly they would look both ways first to check there was nobody around. When he or she failed he would open the window and say it was his.

We used to go to a small pub for our lunch just a few steps away. In the summer just round the corner was Lincoln Inn Fields and we could watch netball being played whilst we ate our sandwiches. One particular day the pub had no sandwiches, but the management said there was a bacon tree close to the bushes in the field. On checking this out several arrows came over the bushes just missing us. We complained at the pub who said he was sorry he meant to say ham bush, Oh dear.

1971

My Company, H A Sandiford & Partners was moving from Holborn in London out into the Country, to save costs in both rates and travelling expenses as well as a nicer environment. We looked to move from Romford to close to Godalming where the firm was settling and put a deposit and exchanged on a house nearby.

Three days after exchanging we were invited to Yvonne's parents. When we arrived, we found her Grandma was there reading teacups – ooh could you read my teacup please – oh, go on then.

Some tea was quickly brewed, after drinking it I had to swill the cup round and pour any liquid into my saucer. Grandma started reading my cup.

You are moving house (she knew that) – it's lovely – sideways onto the road, fronting onto a long drive and it's all white with black beams. No, I'm afraid Grandma you are quite wrong this time, we have actually exchanged on a normal house with a front garden and the road at the front. No, she said you are not moving there. I left it at that as she was obviously wrong.

Unbelievably, a letter arrived 2 or 3 days later from my Solicitor. The house we had exchanged on was being withdrawn from the market – we would be paid all expenses and the owners were offering £50 compensation.

From then on Nana was always right!

So, we are back house hunting. We looked at lots of Surrey villages including Bookham.

In the estate agent's window, there was a cottage just like Nana pictured – we ended up buying it.

Did we buy it because it was just as Nana said or because we liked it? Probably both.

1972

We decide a hotel holiday in Spain, but we will drive there with our 18-month-old baby.

We took an unusual mountain pass back and planned to drive through the night.

Oh dear, the Spanish Border was open, but the French was closed! One could get marooned in no man's land.

The Spanish Border Police could not be more helpful and telephoned the French Border asking if they would be good enough to let us in.

No.

Only answer sleep in the car.
Next morning, we entered France and drove home.

1973

We moved to the cottage in Bookham and our Queen's Jubilee was celebrated by the local Doctor and me doing a Punch & Judy show in the middle of the road.

We decided to hold a Garden Party at home in Bookham inviting a few clients as well as family and friends.

We planned to roast a pig. I ordered the pig from a supplier just along the road to Guildford.

I thought the pig would lay across the back seat which I had covered with newspaper. I had not considered rigor mortis hence the pig would not bend nor fit across the car – only way was to drop the back of the passenger seat down and lay the pig in the front seat. He did look as though he was my passenger – quite a giggle.

Due to road works I was stopped at traffic lights next to a small bus queue – they were talking about the passenger I felt sure.

Prior to this I had 'borrowed' some pipe and fittings from work and made a spit to go through the pig with a handle on the end so we could keep it turning.

I wasn't sure which end of the pig I should push this length of 1" pipe in – I decided 'up its bum' would be easiest but the other end got jammed against its teeth – no problem use more force – poor dead pig, lost its front teeth. It all had to be wired to the spit to make it go round when we turned the handle.

At this time, we were in the midst of the Dutch Elm disease and trees were being felled all over the place. I contacted the Council to see how I could have some of these logs.

I had to sign a form to certify the timber would all be burnt, and I could then send a lorry for a load – no problem borrow the firm's lorry!

I felt that the boss would not say no as he was coming to the party. Anyway, I lit a fire about 8.00 a.m. some 6 foot long. After an hour we had some hot embers and considerable radiant heat.

I didn't worry too much about Stephen Boltzmann formulae to calculate the amount of heat!

Come about 6.00 p.m. the pig was not cooked (tested by a stab-in meat thermometer mounted on a long stick. I decided the meat temperature should be 170°F – the damn pig refused to shift above 155 °F and all the timber is gone.

I knew I was going to have to re-new the front 5 bar gate and post shortly so off they came – and the cooking continued.
Come 7.45 p.m. I decided the pig was cooked. However, Yvonne my wife, insisted I ate some and if I was not ill in ½ hour then it could be served.
I remember at this party, terminal 4 at Heathrow had just opened and was being discussed. Yvonne thought it looked awful.

I went and found Peter and brought him over – I said – Yvonne you must meet Peter – Terminal 4 Architect – what were you saying? I wasn't popular!

About October a phone call from a Ministry Department asked if I could design a large air conditioning installation and have it working by 3rd March the following year. All we knew was that the heat output from the computer equipment that the building would house was 150,000 watts and they did not have a building.

I said I thought it could be done if the on-date was more important than correct procedure. This was agreed and I was put in taxi with a Ministry Property guy who had a list of vacant premises in London and close to the City. I was running in and out of 14 buildings commenting – no won't fit or may do. In the end I selected a building and started designing.

I was concerned that I could not fit all the ductwork required in the plant area, I was working at home late into the night when my wife came down from bed wanting to know why I was working so late – I said I can't fit in all the recirculating ductwork. She said that's easily answered – don't put it in – EXACTLY – she had resolved a problem I had been sweating about for 3 days in 3 minutes – good girl.

The whole plant room became a return air plenum. I now calculated wind speeds rather than ducted air velocities! Having realised I have to make the plant room a Plenum Chamber I required some unusual filters to take the 'room air' into the plant where it would be cooled or heated but with a relatively slow air velocity.

I found the American filter company made just the job so were specified.

I think the Managing Director was trying to get round me. I don't know why as his units were already selected. He had his own airplane and asked me if I and my wife would like a flight. Well, why not.

We had to go to an aerodrome in Redhill where he gave me a map and said 'where is your house? – we will fly over it. Well, this map had no roads or anything else I recognised. So, he gave me a motoring type map and I was able to point to my house.

We took off. "We are over your house now" – no we are not; I don't recognise anything. Then Yvonne who was in the rear seat said, "look that's the Southend Road".

I said oh yes, please turn left at that next roundabout.

The pilot found it quite funny being asked to take the 3rd on the left! Yvonne was most upset that none of our neighbours were in their gardens.

The job was handed over at 11.00 a.m. on 3rd March as promised.

As I mentioned, we moved to Bookham in Surrey but left my parents in Ilford, Essex. Obviously, we wanted to move them to nearer where we now lived. All we required was a bridging loan covering the money between selling and buying. My parents were with Midland Bank, and these were approached for a bridging loan for, I think, £5,000 which in the first place they refused as they didn't think the house they were selling (their security) was worth £5,000. I managed to convince the Manager that it was – they relented and let us have £5,000. However, we could not sell the property for the £5,000 – the only option was to split it into 2 flats – hopefully selling each for £2,500, or more. I went back to the bank for a loan of £6,000 to enable us to split the property into 2 flats.

They said no. I dived in asking if they realised that a now retired Manager had loaned my Father £5,000 against a property not worth £5,000. If you value your honour you will now help us to split the house into 2 flats, we had a builder's quote for the work for £4,400.
They agreed to make the necessary loans. I didn't tell them that I had applied to the Council for a building betterment grant – this was granted.

The whole arrangement worked. We sold the two flats as 100-year leaseholds – such that in 100 years (2075) the properties returned to me. I would have to give up smoking if I wanted to see them back when I reached my 133rd birthday! In the meantime, I was responsible for underground drainage.

I sold the lease in 2014 for the cost of the Solicitors fees.

We are now working on site installing relatively complicated air conditioning which had to maintain 50% Relative Humidity in not only the main computer hall but all other offices for the Post Office (Telecoms Department).

To produce the cooling, I had chosen the very latest "screw" type compressors from America. These were ordered in good time to suit the site program. I will not name the international company who were supplying them, but it was a company I often used for air conditioning components. The Director took a particular interest in this large order, so when I was going to Spain for our annual holiday and our compressors were actually on the high seas I asked the Director (I shall call him Arthur) to keep a very special eye on our compressors – we can't afford for them to be stuck in customs. He promised solemnly that realising how important the compressors were, he would personally check on their progress daily.

Yvonne and I flew to Spain. Didn't like our hotel and checked into a better one. Next day walk to the each. Unbelievable! On the other side of the road was Arthur with a friend! He saw me and disappeared round a corner. I never saw him again on this holiday, although our compressors arrived, I never did business with this company again.

I heard Arthur had recently died from AIDS. I was in a position to place an order for some large equipment to a new Major Insurance Company H.Q. building in London. So, they received it. I just hoped the next Director does not tell lies.

1974

Our second son is born in March. Yvonne was delighted when I told her his eyes were o.k.

We knew we were expecting a boy, so Yvonne had plenty of time to choose a name. I don't know what went through her mind, but James was chosen. Some time later she realised that a famous broadcaster was called James Alexander, and that this was a nice sounding name, so that was that James Alexander was chosen with Winston – a family name, added. Hence James Alexander Winston Pitt. Perhaps partly named after a famous shark.

1975
Age 33

In my trade of heating and air conditioning there is a trend towards design by the contractor instead of the Consulting Engineer designing and the Contractor installing the various services. I was contacted by a firm of Contractor's who wanted to employ a designer. They were offering more money and a COMPANY CAR!

Job accepted and a new car with darkened glass was arranged – wonderful.
I received a request to be a guest lecturer at what is now Surrey University teaching project management. The first time I took a class, at the end of the lessons the entire class clapped, and several said thank you for telling us how to really manage a project! The actual syllabus, I thought was pretty poor with no coverage of what to do when things go wrong. I was pleased I did

not have to follow this silly syllabus.

Correcting wrongs or better still preventing them is what project management is all about. A delivery scheduled for 2.00 pm, 11th March that arrives the next day must not hold anything up – very important.

Critical Path Analysis is also nonsense – every path is critical!
Rarely was I involved in a late or over budget project. Most over budget conclusions are due to inaccurate budgeting in the first place, and they are probably not in fact over the correct budget!

Yvonne and I decide on a holiday in Florida taking in Disneyland. A friend of mine owned a holiday home in Tampa and he agreed to let us borrow it for a week or two.

Tampa is along the Florida Keys – basically a long line of islands connected by bridges or narrow lengths of land.
We were booked on a flight from London Heathrow but at the last minute I was unable to go on the agreed date due to a very important business meeting.

So, I flew the next day, and I was going to Tampa where Yvonne would arrive the day before. I on the plane. I all asleep. I wake up. Wow – just in time – people were getting off of the flight – quick, grab my bag and jacket and go.

I had a long wait for my case to come round. After one and half hours I reported my bag as lost.
Two huge policemen arrived where I was doing the reporting

"Come with us Sir"

Where are you? I'm in Tampa but my luggage seems to have gone missing.

They wanted my name and address and the true reason I had landed at North Carolina.

Oh dear.

It turned out that the plane had made a stopover – perhaps for refueling and I should have stayed on the plane.

I tried to explain what actually happened and surprise he believed me.
The huge policeman pointed out however that it was unlawful to send personal luggage on a plane without the person – I really thought I would be arrested. However, he said "there's a hotel over the road – go there and fly tomorrow".

I went into the hotel but could not see the check-in.

I asked two girls where it was – "wow, are you from New Zealand? No, I'm English".

Oooh, we are at a wedding downstairs, we would love an Englishman to join us.

I wasn't sure if she had the authority to invite me but thought it ok when it came clear that she was the head bridesmaid on their way outside to smoke.

Everybody wanted to talk to me.

The policeman said what I had done was unlawful. If it had been illegal I would be in serious trouble as it is definitely against the law to bring into the country a sick bird especially an ill eagle.

1976

This company was the first in the country to be awarded BS5750 for Quality Assurance, which stood us in good stead resulting in considerable growth and profitability.

My wife thought it would be a good idea to have a daughter, having successfully reared two boys. I wasn't so keen and in the end we decided on a lady dog. We purchased a golden Labrador without a name. We decided to go through the alphabet selecting names that may be suitable. I started at Z and Zoe was quickly agreed.

At this time, I had 2 pet white ducks and Zoe was happy to sit with them instead of eating them. A jolly good thing.

I, Yvonne, and Yvonne's two friends decided to go out for a drink – that's what married people did, then, nowadays they will go out for a meal.

I suggested a particular venue where drinks were served with various snacks. Good idea.

Off we go to the Black Swan. Several minutes, maybe 15 was spent discussing and arguing about what to eat and drink.
I can't remember the actual order, but I remember it was waitress service.

Yes, we are ready to order. Everybody wanted something different, and it probably took the waitress 5 minutes to get it all down correctly – I do remember I had sardines on toast and a nice red wine – I used to drink red wine by the gallon as 'they' said it was good for you – I proved it wasn't! I nearly had to have my leg amputated years later.
I can't blame just the glass I had in the Black Swan though!

Due to the complicated order, the order was going to take some time to fulfil.

Just then the door opened, and a guy walked in with 6 or 7 others – I recognised him – must be somebody I knew?

As he passed a waitress he simply said – 2 bottles and 3 dozen please. Simple, took about 3 seconds.

His Champagne and oysters were sent well before our table was served.

I then realised it was Ton Jones – I said to the other three at our table – that's Tom Jones, they had their back to him – I was the only one who could see – I said I know him, I'll go and bring him over – "NO YOU WON'T, SIT STILL, YOU DON'T KNOW HIM".
They didn't know that I worked on the same building site as him just before he became famous – a new school in Romford, Essex.

I went over to him and introduced myself as Barry – I said Tom –

you won't recognise me, but I remember talking to you in Romford years ago. Could I introduce you to my Wife and her friends – Sure.

He stood up and I turn round – WOW! My table is empty.

Sorry Tom looks like either you or I have frightened them away – He smiled – I think he found it amusing.

It turned out that two suddenly had an urge to the go to the loo and Yvonne, my wife, hid behind a column. I should mention that the Black Swan was a posh place decorated as Roman with I think Corinthian columns and lots of complicated plasterwork. When we were done we had to ask to have the door unlocked to let us out. The evening was good for the book!

1977

I arrived home late; my wife opened the door with a glass of milk – drink this and get to the hospital it's your Father.

I drove at something less than 200 mph.

Dad had pneumonia – doctor and I chatted and decided not to treat him, but would they give me a cylinder of oxygen and mask, but it is not necessary to turn the bottle on. He died shortly after. I felt comfortable with the decision I took.
We decide to go to South Africa where friends of ours now lived. They had a house in Randburg near Johannesburg complete with swimming pool and all that goes with a nice house. At this time white people and black people were, in the main, kept apart – it was called apartheid.

This was a strange idea to me, although everybody read about the situation, but it felt immoral to live it.

Jeff and Janet's maid was a lovely 'black girl' called Helen, and next-door neighbours were Africanas – descended from the Dutch.

The Africanas people seriously thought they were white and quite different from the indigenous black people.

One day Janet asked me to walk to the post office – I wasn't very keen on this idea, but I thought I had better go. When I got there, there were 2 counters and above them were 2 signs "BLACKS" and "WHITES" = I thought I'm not in agreement with this, so I stood in the "BLACK" queue.

Two enormous smiling black guys came over to me, picked me up and put me in the "WHITES" queue. They said, "that's better"!
Back 'home', Janet and Jeff said this was a silly thing to do.

Helen – a lovely girl who worked for Janet and Jeff lived in a wooden hut in the garden. Her door was kept shut (locked) with a hasp and staple. A bent 6" nail was dropped into the hasp to keep it from opening.

I said to Jeff – surely she should at least have a decent lock with a key.

He suggested, with a smile that if I think that then I should fix one. Next time we went to the shops I bought a suitable lock and the next day I fitted it and gave Helen the key.
Unbelievably, 3 or 4 days later she had removed "my lock" and replaced the bent nail system – good job I didn't throw the hasp and staple and the bent nail away. I had left them on a rock close to her hut.

They had a geranium plant in their garden some 7 feet high – I calculated one could get 250 cuttings from it!

We set off to the Kruger Park to see the Jungle and all the animals – Jeff took snake serum with us I was told but I never saw it!

I was map reading.

Now you need to know that in the Park all the animals have right of way and it's illegal to drive after dark – the time this starts is indicated around the park. We are booked into a Holiday Inn Hotel in the park and to get to it one had to take a turning on the left off of the "main" road after the sign "END OF TAR"

As map reader I said turn left in 2 miles – we were now 10 miles past the sign 'END OF TAR".

I should mention that roads do move, if after rain a road has been washed away a new one will be dug quite quickly.

After 10 miles we hadn't seen a turning on the left – we are now getting close to the Mozambique boarder, which was worrying us, according to the English newspapers there is a war on the border. We were considering turning back when just round a corner we had to stop as there was an enormous guy sitting in a deck chair with a large gun in the middle of the road. I got out and went up to him to find out why he was there.

'Passport' he said – it turned out that this was the official South Africa/Mozambique boarder! – no sign of a war other than his automatic gun.

I got chatting – he said we had missed the turning 5 miles back. It was getting dark – we had to get going.
We arrived!

We showered and changed and went to dinner. The boys had had their food earlier and were in bed each with a glass of water.

We took it in turns to check them out every ½ hour.

My turn after an hour – I went up to the room, normally we would just open the door and listen, but something told me to risk turning the light on. Just as well I did. Both of the boy's tumblers of water had a wriggling beetle floating in them – SAME SIZE AS THE TUMBLER.

No bedtime water in Africa!

We were up early and on our way the next morning. We were going to head for a place we would use as our base. On arrival we were shown to our 'roundarval' a 'mud hut' constructed from modern materials and were given a paraffin Hurricane Lamp for light, and a pot if any of us required a pee during the night.

The first day we toured around relatively locally.

I couldn't see much in the way of security to keep us and animals apart except a cattle grid from the road and a 4-foot fence.

One needs to know some animals are not always friendly; these include Lions, Elephants, Buffaloes and Wart Hogs.

At dusk we are restricted to the 'camp' area.

When the dinner drums sounded (about 7,000 decibels) we headed to the restaurant building and were shown to our seats. It was very posh.
Drinks? Oh yes, a bottle of claret and 2 cokes please (I can't remember the name of the wine!).

Our wine came to the table by Concord – very quick – but no cokes. After 10 minutes "WAITER" – 2 cokes please – after another 10 minutes "WAITER" 2 cokes please.
I gave up and went through a pair of doors where the staff were coming and going – are you the manager? "Yes, how can I help" – "I'VE ORDERED 2 COKES 3 TIMES – find them please". As soon as I sat down again 6 cokes arrive.

Lovely.

Next morning us 4 lads were up early and drove to a nearby water hole and observed several species drinking.

On our return, Yvonne was in a deck chair in the field reading just outside our roundaval with 8 wart hogs all around her! – NOT A GOOD IDEA.

We shouted at her to keep still and quiet whilst we got help, however Jeff decided we didn't require help we could shoo them away – we did, but a bit dodgy to say the least.

JOB DONE.

The hotel had a swimming pool cut into the rock. The lads loved it. We then drove onto Shush-Lewi for a period of beach holiday.

We saw three surfers close to several sharks – we shouted 'look behind you' – probably did no good. I'm sure the surfers knew what they were doing.

On the way back to Johannesburg we stopped 2 or 3 times.

At one stop in Zulu Land, we had our fortunes read by a guy in traditional witchdoctor's dress who 'threw the bones (may have been stones)'. He told me I was going to live to over 100. He obviously didn't know that at that time I smoked!

Another stop was closer to home – a snake park. We had not seen any snakes close up. 3 handlers brought out a massive python (they claimed it was the biggest in the world.

"Does anybody want to help hold this snake - I was first there. We will take each end and you will be in the centre with the snake's belly on your shoulders. Another handler will stand close to you – you may require helping due to the heavy weight.

Struth – it was heavy, but I was quite chuffed I managed it on my own.

On arriving back in England, after about 3 weeks a letter arrived from Jeff and Janet in South Africa containing a cutting from their newspaper reporting that that snake had killed its handler!

- Best keep away from big snakes!

1978

I have a phone call from a prominent member of a Middle Eastern Government – could I help him buy a boat – he had been given my name, he said by a friend of mine – when given the name of this friend of mine I confirmed to myself that I had never heard of him.

Following a subsequent phone call he didn't want a boat he needed a ship to meet his requirements. As gambling was illegal in this Country he has a plan to anchor a ship just outside territorial waters as a hotel/restaurant and gaming facility with facilities for taxi type boats to drive into the ship with customers.

I said I would see what I could do but please give proof of funds. I believe I required £15,000,000 for the purchase – this arrived but at a much larger figure.

I had in mind my neighbour Roger, who was a Radio Officer on a big ship – phone Roger.

How did you know it is coming up for sale? – I didn't.

He messaged the Chairman of the Company saying I was in mind to purchase.

My Wife and I were invited to look over the ship the next time she came into port. We were well looked after by the senior crew as well as our friend Roger being with us. Negotiations started and I agreed a price which I wanted to include delivery. There were numerous problems delivering the ship to the Middle East. No worry a slight reduction in price did the trick. We found a qualified Captain who would, at a cost, deliver her for me.

In the meantime, I am producing drawings to turn holds into cabins and an internal 'marina'.

1979

I am invited to become a livery man which I accepted – one is also granted the freedom of the City of London correctly known as a Freeman of the City provided one has been a good guy – one day late payment of your Council Rates (now known as Council Tax) and you have no chance!

To be truly appointed one is clothed in a black robe and sits on the top table of the livery dinner (the only time you do for many years), On taking the Oath of a Freeman at the Guild Hall I was surprised to see the BBC cameras in action as I came out. Alas! A famous band leader, Joe Loss, was made a Freeman at the same time as me and the cameras were pointing at him! The lady from the Daily Mirror made it clear that she had no interest in me at all.

Out of interest the saying that a person who has the Freedom of London can drive sheep over London Bridge is not strictly true. In fact, you can drive animals to market through London – I guess if the route includes London Bridge then the saying is true.

As a Managing Director of Jefferies – employing about 170 people in the group I used to follow the profitability of all projects. It soon became clear that at "completion" most projects were showing the tendered profit.

Then we started losing money – this wasn't working, that wasn't right, and we were forever correcting mistakes and paying to correct them.

Answer– simply agree with the site operatives, fitters, managers, and buyers – all front people how much we will pay them IF the project was correctly finished and on time (not 1 day late).

This worked brilliantly, some fitters were now earning more than me – every project showed its tendered profit. The firm went from strength to strength. More details of this arrangement are given in the Appendices.

BT called saying they wanted a vault to keep documents in good condition for 1000 years.

The world's expert regarding the preservation of paper and mould was based in the British Museum. I didn't go to see him myself but the Senior engineer that went came back with a colourful picture of a small man behind a huge desk holding a pin and pointing out that 4 million spores that turn paper yellow can sit on this pin head. (I think it was 4 million).

I would not live for another 1000 years but we must do our best. It meant very fine tolerances – temperature $16°C$ plus/minus $0.01°C$, humidity 40% plus/minus 1%.

This meant an air-conditioned room within an air-conditioned room. All went well; out of interest we hung 600 mm long mercury in glass thermometers in a grid throughout the room. Our problem was, when we approached one to read it the mercury shot up – we ended up having fewer thermometers and read through binoculars.

Yvonne wanted both boys to go to Millfield School – fortunately both of them were good at football and goal keeping and were granted bursaries – even so the fees did not come cheap. I remember in the 1980's writing out cheques for £20,000 (£55,000 today).

This didn't include endless sports equipment. Worth every penny – provided you have enough pennies!

As soon as they left school I bought a new boat.

1980

I had drifted into Sales & Marketing, which included looking after our Clients. You need to know, to understand this situation, that strawberries were not generally available outside the summer period, although were available to a few top restaurants and hotels who would have them especially flown in.
When I entertained heavyweight Clients, I made sure that Beoty's Restaurant had some strawberries available. I would also arrange for a bottle of Nui St George to be opened an hour or two before we arrived.

One time though I had dined at Beoty's every day for about 5 days with Clients and hence had eaten strawberries every day. One day I had Clients with me who knew me well and I was able to joke with the Waiter that I was fed up with strawberries so how about a baked jam roll and custard?

As things worked out I didn't dine at Beoty's for 2 or 3 weeks, then the opportunity arrived of taking the Chairman and Company Secretary of the Country's largest company to lunch.
How about some strawberries and cream – Oooh yes sounds super. Two desserts of strawberries arrived, and the Waiter said 'yours will follow shortly Mr. Pitt' – strange.

Then <u>wow</u> a huge baked jam roll arrived. I wanted the floor to open!

I had no option but to tell them how I had joked with the Waiter a few weeks before.

Super! They probably still remember this.

1981

I am made a fellow of CIBSE (The Chartered Institution of Building Services Engineers).

1982

I decided to give a lecture in our boardroom outlining how the company worked – we had experts in a department who knew very little about another department. Good idea, and we will film it and all new employees will be shown it.

Oh dear, the guy in charge of the camera didn't have the mike plugged in. We tried to give the lecture again, but it was not a success.
I will let you into some management secrets. I never spoke badly or shouted to any of my staff, but what I did do once or twice a year is hold a phone to my ear somewhere where several staff could hear and shout at 300 decibels saying the guy on the phone (it was always a guy) was an idiot and if I wanted the job done by Friday that is what I meant – you are an idiot and a waste of space – and so I went on and on very loud. Close staff stood there with their mouths open – they didn't know I could do that.
Very soon everyone made sure they didn't upset me.

The other tool is a bit mean. Now we had a rule – I'm at BPA now that the phone had to be answered within a certain number of rings, but I can't recall the number. New rules made it difficult to sack somebody for not answering a phone quickly.
I would pick up my phone and say to the switchboard girl (it was always a girl, but I don't know why) I'm going to make a very important call – please don't interrupt me.

I would then phone the company and ask to speak to Mr. Pitt – sorry he cannot be disturbed just now. But I must speak to him now it's a matter of extreme importance – she would interrupt me, and I would shout 'TOLD YOU NOT TO INTERRUPT ME' – this is very serious – I'm coming round straight away.

The poor girl couldn't cope and left us. This only happened once when our switchboard was not answered for numerous rings and her attitude was not welcoming to Clients. I probably should not have told you this.

It would be far too dangerous to learn to sail by me outlining what to do in this book, but this is when I started sailing lessons.

Sign up for sailing lessons – these split into two types:

Land based – rather like school and probably taught in a school classroom during evenings and

Afloat based - when you board perhaps with 2 or 3 others and a box comes too. What's in the box? Exciting.
Answer – your food for a week!

The captain/skipper/teacher will organise you all such that everything from steering to washing up is shared fairly.

One important thing you learn is to recover a 'man overboard' – that's what we shout even if it's a lady. Skipper appoints somebody to do absolutely nothing except point at the person in the water.

Best not to practice with a real person.
An artificial person consists of a fender (a blow-up rubber sausage hanging over the side of your boat when mooring (nautical parking) tied with a short length of rope to a bucket.

The skipper will throw this overboard and shout 'man overboard practice'. Whoever is steering at the time must turn the board round and get back alongside the bucketed fender, It gets a little more complicated as you want the wind to blow the boat onto the person (fender) not the opposite.

When taking an exam, twice I could not get back to pick up the fender – a certain failure of the exam.

Half an hour later I was still steering, and my hat blew off.
I turned the boat round, stopped with my hat on the port (left hand side) and the wind blowing onto the starboard side.

I passed the exam.

Another tip is to learn how to tie knots, especially a Bowline.

Just remember the rabbit (short end of the rope) comes up to the hole, (a loop in the long end of the rope) goes round the tree (the main part of the rope for a bowline) and then goes back down the hole.

I always recall my dear friend J.C. up the bow of the boat (the front) in a roughish sea getting soaking wet, loudly shouting "up the hole round the tree back down hole" – The anchor was secured.

I went to the boat show at Olympia and went across a huge sign "houses for sale". They were shown as models and formed a Marina with each house having its own pontoon (landing platform) where one could keep their own boat.

They were going to be built at Hythe near Southampton. They looked beautiful and decided there and then to buy one – I said to a guy on the stand that I would like to buy that one – pointing to the one on the model right opposite the lock which was the way in and out to the sea. Is that one sold – no, none are sold yet. I got my cheque book out and made out a cheque for £12,000, this being 10% of the quoted (on a large board) price – I asked who I make the cheque out to – he said I couldn't buy it yet because it wasn't built – I said irrelevant, I want to buy it and it says on the wall "houses for sale" – we argued for a few minutes and then gave up. Some 3 weeks later I realised why I couldn't buy it – they were just testing the market allowing the price to go up. I can't remember what I finally paid but it was probably £25,000 more than the quote at the boat show.

We employed an internal designer to decorate and select furniture. We had 3 floors, and I wanted the top bedroom to be an office and decorated in yellow such that we could call it the yellow room.

I think the cost was £14,000 or £40,000 – can't remember.

We sold and purchased 3 houses in this Marina moving up in the market each time.

When it was decided to sell, I didn't get any interest at the price I wanted. I placed the following advertisement in the local paper as well as the Surrey Advertiser:

"Millionaires kit for sale"

4 bed house in Hythe Marina, almost new, 34-foot yacht, 14' speed boat. 4.2 litre jaguar car, grey inflatable, lots of others" - £600,000

This was seen by the BBC who wanted to make a programme on executive housing.

"Would you please attend the house at 2.00 pm Monday with your wife"? I said yes even though my wife was now living in America. No problem my right-hand man Pam (a super girl who was called a secretary) was requested to come with me and pretend to be my wife – we also took Zoe our golden Labrador.

All rooms were furnished as well as the yacht and we had to walk the dog up and down the road for their cameraman.

I never saw the programme, if indeed, they ever made one. I never got any interest to my advertisement either.

In the end the boat was sold to a local boat leasing company, I think for
£46,000. All of this money was paid into BPA Consultants bank to help with the cash flow problems they were having.

We were contacted by an official of the Mauritius Government which become independent from Britain in 1968 having been governed by us since 1810. "How can I help you"? – well, one half of our country is wet and the other very dry, we thought a big pipe from one end to the other may be a good idea.

Several meetings and phone calls later we had a drawing of a suitable pipeline, proposed lakes, pumps and other things.

The pumps were going to be enormous and there was not sufficient power available to power them.

Although a little longer than a direct route, our pipe followed a main North/South road to ensure good access and security.

To cut a long story short, our pipelines above ground were a tourist attraction!

1983

Having just moved into Uplands, one of the first jobs was to insulate the loft (roof space today) and due to the complicated shape and non-standard joist spacing, I opted for pea size granular insulation.

First job was to get the sacks upstairs and then I started opening the sacks and tipping the insulation between the joists.

Some rooms had 'SCILLINGS' – sloping ceilings coming down the walls and following the slope of the roof.

One area to fill was the sloping joists and several bags went down between the joists – I followed with the rest of the roof.

When all was finished Yvonne went to the airing cupboard and virtually got totally covered in insulation beads - I had filled the cupboard from above without knowing it!

In the accounts department at Jefferies there was one of the nicest guys. He was from Sri Lanka and called Bala. I was shopping for something quite different when I came across a giant teddy bear. I've got to buy this – let's think who can I give it to for Christmas which was coming up.

I had heard that Bala had a little daughter – so that's it – a big Teddy is her Christmas present.

I understand that she loved her new Teddy and used to sit in a corner of a room with it/him/her.

Several months later I heard that the ceiling fell down in the room where she was sitting, the height of the bear saved her from injury – who knows maybe it saved her life!

Came across a small restaurant in Holborn and took a client there for lunch. The service was terrible, and the waitress was useless, shouting at me. I came back "I'll buy this place and sack you".

I found out who owned the restaurant – contacted him and low and behold he was looking to sell.
I bought it for £12,000. My wife took her best friend for a lunch to see what could be done. The waitress was not sacked but she changed her attitude to me.

Somebody I didn't know was already interested in the purchase, but I found out later that he was argumentative; however, I sold it to him for £14,500. My Solicitors charged £1,800.

I had an early Monday morning knock on my door (I had got in early at 6.30) and a guy called Louis rushed in looking as white as a ghost, shaking, and could barely speak – he was in a terrible state.

As you know Barry, I have joined the Freemasons and during the weekend I found out that as a Catholic I can't be a Mason. Rubbish, yes you can – No No I really can't – I've come to see you to ask how I go about resigning – who do I write to, what do I do? I must leave.

As Master of the Lodge, you can just tell me you want to resign – 'I want to resign' he said. Louis you are no longer a member, an incredible calm came over him and could not thank me enough!

Talking about Freemasonry, I was Master of my Lodge Chapter 3 times or as we say, 'in the chair'. On the first occasion it was necessary for my wife Yvonne to give a speech at the Ladies Night which was going to be held in March.

Bless her she was actually practicing her speech on the beach the previous summer. Her speech went down well, and we had a good evening. Our dark red Jaguar car was in for a service. Yvonne and I got a lift back to the main dealer to collect it on the Thursday as agreed.

The staff offered us a coffee – no thanks, just here to collect my car.

After about ½ an hour what looked like a senior manager came over to us and explained that my car had been stolen during the night – he offered a courtesy car – Oh well we looked at each other – it's insured, we will get another one – then 3 policemen arrived.

I was just driving off when Yvonne shouted stop, got out and ran back to the police. "You must find our car it's got my tapes in it!
The police did very little about finding it but believe it or not I found it. The number had been altered with black tape! – Yvonne's tapes were still in it!

1984

I was working for Standard Chartered Bank, our contact being a guy called Stan at practical level although I got to know board level managers. I was known as an amusing individual who normally had a trick up his sleeve and a story to tell.

The Chairman of the bank usually took the cleaners out for a Christmas Lunch and always invited me to keep everybody amused. As a member of the Wig & Pen Club, the owner, Joe Coral's son, liked to entertain European MP's when in Town and invited me to the lunches – again to keep all amused.

Most of the stories I told were true or looking back may be roughly 99.3142% true.

When we first moved in to our first house in 1967 the quickest way to the bus stop was to balance across a scaffold board traversing a small stream.

Coming home one night earlier than normal I encountered a dead pony on the pavement with several people around it – I was asked if I could lend a hand, apparently they wanted to not only get it into the house but up the stairs as well.

It was very heavy but between us we managed. The owner of the house then wanted the pony to put into the bath – why?

It turned out that the owner's brother was coming that evening and he was a big-headed guy who always claimed to know everything.

The owner knew he would go upstairs on arrival and come down asking if I knew there was a horse in the bath and the owner would be able to reply, "I KNOW", which made his day.

CAD (Computer Aided Design) was becoming available to our engineering fraternity; we required high-resolution screens. In 1984 we had to pay £5,000 per screen (£17,000 today). We built up to 8 screens and then in 1988 moved the CAD facilities into a separate company called WOCAD.

About 1987 I was very worried about a senior staff member who was constantly thirsty and would gulp down 2 or 3 pints of bitter at lunch time. I insisted he see his doctor, but he refused.

One way out of this was for the company to pay for every employee to have a Medical. He had to go to this.

The same day as the medical he had a phone call to contact his GP urgently.

He was found to be diabetic and could have lost a leg (or more) if not treated. He has followed a careful diet regime ever since.

He was a Senior Engineer and also the CEO of QA Services Ltd but also arranged our transport including buying me new cars from time to time.

One car he suggested I had was a jaguar XJS with a long bonnet, the follow on from the 'E' type Jag. This car was delivered about 6.00 pm whilst I was chairing an important meeting. The delivery guy insisted on talking to me through the car – "GO AWAY I'm busy". I had to shout to shut him up.

About 9.30 pm the meeting finished, I found the key to my new car, locked up the office and got into new dark red car and guess what, the hand brake was jammed on – wouldn't release.

Grrrr – had to get a taxi home. Next day transport guy is not popular. His defense was that I should have listened to the delivery guy who would have explained that the car was fitted with a fly off hand brake – you just hit it and it's off!

Our neighbours in Woking who became very friendly, and my wife Yvonne became infatuated with the guy, returned to America and we were invited to a party at their U.S.A. place. The house was set in glorious countrywide in an area where a lot of service personnel lived including pilots, some of which could not tell us what they flew as it was top secret.

Getting involved in a conversation (from memory) with 2 guys and 4 girls we were discussing pilots and flying when 2 of the girls said they were nuts on TOP GUN and had seen the film 3 times (true).

I knew something they did not know – the Top Gun pilots who did all the stunt flying were at the party, as one of them lived virtually next door.

I located him and told him about the two girls. It wasn't long before he came back wearing his helmet and with the second pilot and I took him over. "Girls, you must meet the real Top Gun pilots". Wow, they burst into tears with excitement and probably wet their knickers too (I had no evidence of this)

A very happy 2 girls at Roger's party.

I learned a few things at this party but maybe I am putting 2 and 2 together and making 17?

I'm not sure how many intercontinental and other missiles America has, but these two guys at the party each had a missile! – it wasn't his, but he was charged to ensure it was properly looked after.

There were some huge cars in the road at the party – I wandered whose they were.
Back to the UK and having been away for a 2-week holiday I returned to work early on the first day back – I am now Chairman of the Company; I should mention when a young lad stopped me going into my Office. You can't go in there that's Mr. Pitt's office – but I am Mr. Pitt. I don't recognise you in any case they all say that.

A few moments later another member of staff arrived and told the new lad that I was Mr. Pitt.

I called the new young lad into my office later in the day – I'm sure he thought he was going to get a bollocking – but guess what, I gave him a rise!

He was the type of guy and girl we wanted, 2 years later he was made Apprentice of the Year – he was going to be presented with this award at our annual dinner. I heard he was concerned as he did not have a suit to wear – no problem we bought him one – another happy employee.

Seriously considered building a significant Model. I still had in mind to start more Model Engineering.

I thought a locomotive with lots of stuff that goes up and down around the wheels – the most complicated I could find was 'Bridget' having 4 big wheels and 2 little wheels at the back – professionally known as a 7 ¼" 0-4-2 loco – the 7 ¼" being the distance between the rails. One or two had been made to date including one that was working on a model railway in Wales (I believe) which could pull 30 people on passenger trucks.

I am told that the one I made now sits in a glass case in a pub near Hampton Palace. I named her 'Winston' after my middle name.

Returning to my Model Engineering wish, I purchased the drawings for Bridget – looked at the drawings and could not believe my eyes – the main side frames were 1/4" (6 MM) thick steel – this isn't model engineering this is heavy engineering! And I had to drill 1" (25 mm) diameter holes!

I borrowed a huge 1" drill – but of course it would not fit into my drilling machine chuck – never mind it will go into the main chuck on my lathe sideways.

Some woodwork arranged a support to push the drill into the steel side frames – all done.

Loads more holes to drill and to make sure each side was the same, I temporarily bolted them together and drilled through both of them together. I had the boiler made for me by Cheddar Models from copper.

After some 8 years of work Bridgit was all finished, painted in Brunswick Green (the correct name for British Racing Green). The Brass dome was so shiny, sunglasses are worn by those that look at her.

The CEO of McLarens fancied a model steam locomotive on display in his office. The Surveyor he was using whilst considering the new Woking establishment was also a friend of mine – could he borrow my Bridget.

Quite an honour I thought so we delivered it to him after giving it another good clean and polish. What I didn't know until he moved into his new office that he put it into his 'works' where all the motion gear (the stuff that goes up and down by the wheels was all taken apart, cleaned even more, polished and put back together again.

Not many people know or even believe that McLaren's Engineers are now specialists in coal burning steam engines.

When I finally sold her, I explained that her new name was McLaren Bridget. In 1993 she was shown at the Model Engineers Exhibition in the loan section. I like to think the McLarens connection put between £10 and £5,000 onto the price. Currently similar engines sell for £8,000 to £10,000.

She took about 10 years to build including a gap of 4 years.

When Managing Director of Jefferies', we held Christmas Dinners for our Clients and Staff often catering for 150.
Various venues were used including the main dining area in the House of Commons whose correct name is Palace of Westminster.

One year one of our Managers asked if he could propose the Loyal (some say Royal) toast and I agreed. Unfortunately, having toasted the Queen he went on to say what a wonderful woman she was – speaking for several minutes. I was not happy.

Unbelievably, the next year he asked if he could propose the toast again. Having learned of his mistake last time I agreed, instructing him not to go on about the queen. He stood up and said, "The Queen and the M.D. says the less said about her the better"! That wasn't the idea.

One year we held it on the top floor of Fortnum and Mason. I couldn't believe it when several Chefs carried in a baron of beef which appeared to consist of a whole cow – it was enormous.

At all our Christmas lunches the Chairman and I, and other Directors stood at the door welcoming every guest. The reason we employed apprentices was so a well-dressed lad could keep us fed with gin and tonics at the door.

Whilst thinking of Christmas I am reminded that when operating BPA our more important clients who had become friends and senior staff all received a Harrods's Hamper. I think they were all very appreciative. – I didn't get one, and another thing, I went to the stationery cupboard to steal a roll of sellotape to deal with the wrapping at home and there was NONE LEFT – already all stolen. The following year all members of staff received a roll of sellotape with my compliments.

1985

Having holidayed in Salcombe for a few years and got to like the village, I decided to buy a yacht and paid £12,000 for SUDI, a 30-foot single mast yacht.

We never went very far but in July 1986 we sailed from our berth in Salcombe to Dartmouth. We had on board Yvonne Pitt, Tony and Pam Hall, Eileen Bales and Allan Wood. We left at 8.00 a.m. and arrived at 11.40 a.m. having covered 12 nautical miles. We returned to home port at 5.35 p.m.

I used to frequent the Salcombe sailing club for lunch and a drink often meeting a guy I shall call Malcolm. A rule of most sailing clubs including Salcombe, is discussing work is banned so I never knew what Malcolm did for a living. One day, however, I met him in an ordinary pub, and we were able to talk.

He had several property ideas which I found interesting and developed proposals for several. One of his possibilities was a

400-acre site – the airport owned by Westland Helicopters. We put in a bid of £7 million to purchase it Westland decided to call Tendered bids – us being one of I think 4 bidders.

We bid £7 million plus 10% of any profits made but arranged a leak around the 'trade' that we had bid £7 million in line with our first offer.

Together with one other partner I asked Pete Marwick (our accountants) to form a PLC and placed the necessary £50,000 capital into a new bank account. The company was going to be called Coastal & Countryside Properties PLC.

The purchase included all fittings and fixtures which meant we would suddenly own a club house with top quality snooker table and 2 helicopters. The current owner claimed the helicopters were not fixtures and was planning to fly them out ASAP.

We won. The only problem now was that we did not have £7 million!

I decide to buy the Bank Manager lunch. I could muster £2 million so was looking for £5 million. He thought he may know somebody who could be interested in investing and a meeting was arranged for a few days' time. The guy I shall call 'G' plus his son, and an Advisor arrived, and I was able to outline the proposals the outline of which went as follows:

About 400 acres of land, 300 acres for housing.

A runway requiring re-surfacing that landed a 747 some years earlier and was a bomber base during the War.

Considerable hangers in reasonable condition, control tower complete with radio and radar equipment.
Close to M5 – commenced negotiations with a view of getting our own new junction off of the M5.
Close to main line railway – negotiations commenced re future branch line into our site.

It was agreed that we would agree to a Joint Venture arrangement but initially his company would lend us £5 million to enable the purchase to be made.

I liked the idea of writing a cheque for £7 million (over 20 million now) but my solicitor preferred electronic transfer.

Westland Airport is now in our sights, and we quietly commenced negotiations necessary to produce a state-of-the-art transport interchange including road, rail, and air, bearing in mind a seaport is not too far away.

As far as roads were concerned, our own junction off of the M5 would be ideal, if not maybe a new very large roundabout just off of the M5.

We require a Traffic Engineer; I was surprised to acquire a book listing hundreds of suitable qualified traffic engineers.

I reduced the book to 3 and interviewed the three. I need to tell you that my nearest larger town, Woking, had just been re-trafficked and included what I thought were awful one-way systems and lots of elements I did not like.

At the start of each of the three interviews I opened by saying I'll tell you now if you engineered Woking Town Centre you have no chance of working with me.

One of the three stood out with some brilliant ideas.

I ended up writing to him (his company actually) agreeing terms and provided the project proceeded they would be appointed Consultant.

He replied, thanking me for the contract – "by the way I was responsible for the design of Woking's new road layout"!

Oh well.

I ended up paying him, I think, £45,000 for preliminary design of our own branch off of the M5. British Rail, at that time, did all their own design but we did agree in principle our own siding.

Bristol Airport would be pleased (at a price) to cover all airport operation requirements.

The entire complex would consist of latest facilities state of art such that aircraft could taxi right up to the depots and it would be called "EURO-FLY PARK".

Negotiation commenced with Parcel Force.

One morning I received a telephone call from my solicitor that Mr. G was on his way to the Chancery Court wanting his money back now and did not want a Joint Venture.

I was not happy.

I immediately contacted a friend of mine who was a senior Barrister as well as a Recorder.

We requested a 7-day adjournment to arrange re-payment. We decided to sell the site hoping for a profit.
Who wants to buy our airport?

A well-known individual telephoned saying he had heard on the radio that CCP now owned the airport, and he might like to buy it.

I met him and his small team in London, but we were unable to agree a price. After an hour or so I suggested I should leave.

Just getting into a taxi outside his office a young lady caught my arm and said that her boss had changed his mind.

I went back to his office and shook hands at the figure I had first put.

Things then got complicated; he could not complete it until CCP owned it outright without a court case hanging around. Our bank knew somebody looking at placing up to £10 million. He agreed to lend CCP £5 million to settle the loan.

Out of the blue somebody via a Lawyer claimed that King John had given the site to his family in perpetuity. Oh dear. My Lawyer, after some thinking time recommended that we pay them off, as, although we could most probably prove he had no claim it would take more time than we had available to us.

We paid him £300,000.00 to go away.

We attended the Chancery Court knowing my solicitor now had £8 million in his bank to deal with whatever came up.

The original owner was there to claim their 10% of profits. This was calculated and paid for there and then. All was carried out inside rooms and both parties asked the Judge to approve the agreements we had made. This he did.

Stan, who had previously lived and worked in Lagos, Nigeria for Standard Chartered Bank was asked to take care of Chief Franco who was visiting the Bank.

He introduced him to me. I was surprised to see him in his fabulous gold robes with hat and Staff.

He suggested I should get involved in working in Nigeria as a now growing economy. I flew to Lagos.

I arrived in Lagos and was met off the airplane by Chief Franko, my passport being checked via the car window – we were on our way to the Acquii Hotel where we were booked in and enjoyed a beer with several other people he wanted me to know including an Accountant and Lawyer who would form a company as a branch as C J Jefferies, England.

Although at this time I was Managing Director in England I was limited to what I could agree unless the Chairman and Principal Shareholders also agreed – the Chief Engineer was also there.

Come 10 p.m. after a super meal my Chairman said he was off to his room for the night, I was still with the Bank's engineer. Chief had left perhaps £100-00 in Nira – a wad about 2" thick of 1 Nira notes. My engineer friend suggested we went to the Lower Ground Floor Bar. Wow – on entry it was packed solid with hundreds of young girls, it wasn't long before we were snuggled up to a few of them and then went back to our rooms.
I'm a naturist and it seemed appropriate to suggest we all take our clothes off. I have never seen girls get their clothes off so quickly –

anything to please I guess.

It's a pity my pen has just run out and can't write about the fun that ensued. Room Service was superb.

Next day I found a new pen.

I decided this could be a dodgy place if you didn't know what you were doing but soon made friends mainly with those involved in the Bank.

There were several rules – never go to Victoria Beach – you may never be seen again.

If you see what appears to be a body by the road don't go over to look at it – you may be charged with the cost of burial.

My Chairman and I decided to form a company in Lagos and brought in a Lawyer to assist. There was a chance of work at the bank and for the Government.

Our second visit consisted of a meeting in front of the entire Parliament. I was asked by the Prime Minister, "how many ex-pat permits will you require?" – 5 I replied – "we were approved to start a company and granted the 5 ex-pat Visas.

After the meeting, a well-known world class company approached us – would I sell them some of our ex-pat quotas as they were only granted 2 but wanted 15. Soon after there was a coup, and we abandoned the whole idea.

When our taxi dropped us back to the Icoyi Hotel I notice my case on the pavement then Bob my Chairman noticed his. It turned out that the hotel had forgotten there was an important team arriving and cleared out 2 floors to accommodate them. What do we do?

There was no international telephone except at the telephone office – you went in, queued up to wait for a cubicle to be free. You then entered the cubical having given the reception the number you wanted, and you were put through.
We would visit the local club controlled by a Prince. This club had a toilet in a separate building with dodgy lighting – I was in there

once with an enormous beetle flying about when the lights went out – I nearly died, it was pitch black.

Antoms was the place to eat as it was one of the few air-conditioned restaurants – you could always work out who had dined there as they would spin their glasses round to de-mist them when coming out.

I knew where the Chief Engineer of the Bank lived and wheeled our cases down a road we were told never to walk down at night, and he was happy to accommodate us for the night – we were flying home the next day anyway.

One had to stand in a straight line at the airport otherwise you were pushed into line with the butt of a gun.

Wow – I'm home.

I decided to build an Aviary – I had about 20 larch poles delivered and several rolls of 15mm x 15mm square wire netting. The whole thing on completion was quite big and I decided large enough to house pheasants and/or peacocks.

The Aviary was virtually finished except for the house to give the bird's shelter especially in winter so I ordered 3 peacocks, 1 male and 2 females. Three days later my wife came running to where I was laying out on a couch with a bad back saying she has Woking Station on the phone saying there was a consignment of pigeons for me. I had not ordered any pigeons. I got to the phone and asked the Station Master if he could look into one of the breathing holes to see how big the pigeons were.

He came back so say they were huge. Got it. The peacocks had arrived and there was still no roof on the Aviary shed.

We collected the peacocks, got back home and Yvonne managed to get the roof into position and tied it down for now. A fence panel was used, it would leak if it rained but would at least keep the peacocks inside.

They had to have cornflakes for breakfast (no sugar or milk).
The big plan with peacocks is to have just one perch close the roof as they only scream when they stretch their neck straight up!

My perch location should keep them quiet providing I could put them away every night.

This was quite a fight for the first month or two. As the weather was warm, I started fighting with them without my shirt on as a skin bite or scratch could be dealt with, but a ripped shirt was only suitable for the bin and didn't/t please Yvonne.

Many months went by, and they never screamed.

However, we attended a dinner in London and got back home very late. All was quiet so I decided not to disturb them. Five o'clock in the morning we had a screaming peacock that sounded so loud as though it was in our bedroom. Later that day I went to the bottom of the garden where I seldom visited and unbelievably the new lady next door was just the other side of the fence – "are you Mr Pitt" – "Yes" = "ooo did you hear that owl in the night it was so loud". "Yes I did, I think it must be a rare species as I haven't heard one like that before"! They were put away every night from then on.

I had a trio of silver pheasants which I was hoping to breed. Several nest boxes were made (about 2 feet long x 10" wide x 12" high with a half open 'end'.

Arriving back home from work one evening, on checking the birds, I noticed a pheasant egg on the ground just in front of the door! Wow!

I had hidden the nest boxes under bushes, so I had to crawl around to see if there were eggs in the boxes – THERE WERE – WOW again.

They must have been laid by both hens over several days, but I didn't notice.
I ran indoors to tell Yvonne. She thought they didn't look like silver pheasant eggs but another type of pheasant – how would she know that. No computers to ask then so out came the books. Yvonne was right! So how did they get there?

It was several hours later that Yvonne admitted liability. She was at the Butchers and found him about to throw a tray of small eggs into the bin – Stop! – can I have them please? You can't eat them, and she had to explain her plan, after which he gave them to her. A joy good laugh!

Two boys at Millfield School does not come cheap especially when they are both boarding.

At the end of term, we would drive down to Street in Somerset to collect them and their school trunks (big lockable boxes) and their tuck boxes (smaller lockable boxes). This meant having a big truck or in my case a Range Rover.

We nearly always stopped at a Happy Eater on the way back and a Farm Shop for eggs.

We were always fascinated with the pigs in the field on the right as we drove along the lane towards the actual Farm Shop. Sometimes a huge pig we named Wilf, even though she was a lady, and a mum would be close to the fence, and we always stopped to look as it was missing a back leg – but she seemed to get around ok.
We always enquired in the shop about this pig but the girls serving could never help.

Once, it was apparent to us that the farm owner was serving so I asked him why she only had 3 legs. After 5 minutes explaining I wished I hadn't asked, however he replied in great detail that I won't bore you, but he explained that a few years ago she had saved his (the farmer) life – pulling him out of the barn when tons of bales of hay had fallen on him and pulling him out of the pond when the bank was so slippery he couldn't get out. I interrupted – yes but why has she only go 3 legs?

He then started again how fantastic this pig was.

I interrupted again – YES BUT WHY HAS SHE ONLY GOT 3 LEGS? Well, if you had a pig as clever as that would you eat it all at once?
We left mesmerised forgetting to pay for our eggs – at the end of the drive we turned around and went back to pay. It was now a young lady in the shop who confirmed that the tale the owner had told us was true although she had only worked there 3 weeks.

1985ish

Used a bar in London, both lunchtime and occasionally evenings, and noticed a young lady I thought I recognised, on approaching her she thought she recognised me but neither of us could think why this was so.

However, after a few future meetings it became apparent that she used to work at Millfield School – the School which both of my sons attended – we can only think we must have bumped into each other there. Her name was Joyce but known as JoJo. When Yvonne, my wife fell in love with an American guy, I found I became fonder of Joyce! We are still good friends.

My son James was selected to drive in a national go-cart race to be held in Blackpool.

The cub troop who was sponsoring this was run by an Engineer who was clearly an expert on go-carts.

He won! He has a certificate to prove it. NATIONAL CHAMPION.

1986

A friend of the Chairman (I am now Managing Director), wanted to know if we could design and install all services for a 130-bed total hospital in 1 year. I said yes. This was for an American private hospital company. Their requirement was that the design and installation must be by separate companies. To 'get round' this it was decided that I would form Barry Pitt Associates (BPA) to carry out the design and the contracting side of the company would install – this was agreed. The hospital was completed on programme and at agreed cost.

BPA became known for the design of hospitals and the contracting company known for quality installation of services. Some 30 hospitals and revamping of hospitals followed.

I was now earning £177,273 per year (£254,000 today) of which in one particular year I took a salary of £103,138.

So, it was time to bring in the Senior Engineers as Associates and give them a share of the profit all assuming they would bring in work enabling the company to grow.

I proposed that the new Associates should be on a package of £30,000 per year to encourage them to bring in their own work:

Salary	£22,000
Car Value	£ 4,000
Private Medical Value	£ 2,000
Pension Value	£ 2,000
	£30,000

Some months later we began to run out of money, and I couldn't work out why, until I realised that the new Associates had been put on a Salary of £30,000, some £8,000 more than I had planned giving them a total package of £38,000.00.

On top of this our accountants suggested the Associates shared £111,829 of the profits but I did not agree due to the high level of their pay.

We had just arrived at Ascot – all dressed up in our top hats and the girls in their best frocks, when a lovely gipsy girl came up to me to sell me some lavender and tell me my fortune. I paid £2 to have my fortunate read – I said never mind about that, who is going to win the first race, she went on about how my son was a doctor! In the end she gave me the name of a horse – I can't remember the horse's name but let's say Poppy.

Off she went.

I went back to my party, what did she say – not much – who's going to win the first race – don't know but she said Poppy. I didn't back Poppy – all 11 of the others did and they all won!

Having given all the 6 girls £50.00 each to bet with it became clear that everybody had won something except me. I had not one at all. They were all very sad for me. Unbeknown to all the others I put £1.00 to win on every horse in the race – so whoever won I could cheer and jump up and down.

Everybody was pleased when I won at last.

We all went home very happy after enjoying the 'last night of the proms' type music. All the guys threw their top hats into the trees – a few of us didn't – we were those who owned their own hats.

Moss Bros. send tree climbers to retrieve the hats on the following morning. A great time was had by all.

1987

In May I purchased a new Yacht. It was 34 feet long, all fitted out and delivered for £50,000.00. Our first trip was from Salcombe to Dartmouth.
At Salcombe we would, from time to time, have visits from seals and basking sharks. The boys could motor out to the occasional shark and give it a pat. It seemed to enjoy this. At first I was worried but soon realised he/she was harmless. These sharks can grow to 39 feet (12m) long and filter 2000 tons (50,000 gallons) of water per hour to collect sufficient food for this enormous fish.

It is a protected species in British territorial waters since 2007 and listed as a threatened species.

We decided to tie up with an engineer I shall call Doug. I met Doug, who assured me he could get work in Ghana but just now he had short time cash flow problems – no problem I paid for a trip to Ghana.

On his return he told me the following, but I have no other evidence.

The Prime Minister was of Scottish descent and enjoyed making models of airplanes from plastic kits.

One evening he opened a new kit only to find all the instructions were in Japanese!

He was not happy, so he demanded the presence of the Japanese Ambassador to his office.

The Ambassador arrived and was told to translate as the Prime Minister glued the pieces together. I am told he had to stay all night.

The next day the Prime Minister banned the import of kits where the instructions were in a foreign language!

The Prime Minister wanted to see my original certificates of qualifications – he still has some of them!

It's who you know.

I was looking to move into larger offices in Woking and the Solicitors are taking ages to deal with a simple moving in arrangements and contract.

One evening I was dining at a Livery Dinner (I am a member of the Feltmakers Livery Company). I struck up a conversation with the guy on my left and my wish to move into Woking came up." Where do you want to move to"? I cannot remember the name of the building now but when I mentioned to him the name of the offices, incredibly he said, "well I can help you now – I own that building"!

Handing me his card he said "come round tomorrow about 11.00 and I'll give you the keys! We can catch up with the contract later". We soon moved in.

One of my wife's Yvonne's friends 'owned' a box at Ascot Race Venue and was not planning to use it this year including Ladies Day. "May we borrow it"? – "Yes of course".

Brilliant.

My right-hand man Sally was to organise our day. I think we took 12 all together and Sally put together a very high-quality meal including Champagne, lobsters, and strawberries.
The room and table was decorated with our name BPA emblazoned everywhere. I was wondering what the cost might be. Each lady was given an envelope with £50.00 in it to enable them to place bets.

"Let's go down to the track side" a guest suggested – good idea!

One of our party knew the way and we all followed him.

Wow!

I was staggered to see that Sally had arranged for all the name boards above the ticker tack men to have 'BPA' emblazoned in red on them – good heavens Sally, how much did this cost?

I didn't like to discuss this in front of our guests – some were also Clients. Several hours later I discovered that BPA on these boards was evidence that they complied with the Betting Protection Act!

1988

By now we are regularly sailing to France and the Channel Islands. As our new boat was now registered as a British Ship I was allowed to keep a gun on board. I decided to get a quality one which produced a little flag painted 'bang' on it when fired.

BPA was now separated from the contracting company.

BPA were capable consultants, designing significant projects.

I competed for the design of the Land area Services of the Channel
Tunnel and hence as Senior Partner and owner when we won the contract for design I became Chief M&E Engineer for the Tunnel project.

I had formed a company called QA Services Ltd and our expert knowledge of quality assurance arrangements assisted us in landing the contract. We would have 30% of our staff dealing with QA procedures on the Tunnel.

Kept getting a 'bad back' – nothing wrong according to X-Rays – must be muscular. My Chairman recommended acupuncture – a Chinese Girl in a very expensive flat in London.
I had needles pushed into me all over the place, but interestingly none in the back but felt nothing. Some of the needles she wiggled around and some she tied old leaves around and set fire to them!

I suggested she check the date on her fire insurance before she does anymore! After what seemed like hours but probably only one, having taken ages to get onto her couch I got off – no trouble at all – all pain had gone.

I was in a good mood. I got a taxi to the magic shop in Holborn and bought a fake safety pin. You could push this onto your nose such that it looked as though it was pinned through it!

I drove home and even though I had a key I rang the bell to bring Yvonne to the door – having clipped the safety pin through my nose and held a handkerchief over my nose. On opening the door, she said "how did you get on"? – fantastic but, on removing the handkerchief I said I have to wear this for 4 months – NO! – surely not – well I'm not going out with you I'd rather you have back ache. Well, that's nice I thought.

This Chinese lady had totally mended by back.

Stupidly I did some digging in the garden the next day which brought some of the pain back but not too bad. Back at work as well!

My sons, Antony, and James were goalkeepers whilst at Millfield School.

Scouts watched them, resulting in a Scholarship for Virginia University being offered to Antony, who were keen to build a soccer (USA for football) team. Brilliant, look at the fees I would save – the Scholarship was totally free of charge, but he decided against the idea.

He also had a 3-day trial for Chelsea to become a professional footballer.

During the Summer Holidays, some years Antony lived on our yacht in Salcombe, earning money doing any work that was around.

He also made some cash teaching water skiing. His method was nice and easy so everybody he taught ended up skiing. Other than 'get into water' the only words told to the student were don't bend your arms.

- Now do what I say.

He would pull them along whilst the skis were vertically poking out of the water, gradually getting faster.

He would then shout, 'stand up now'. They always did – and wow they were skiing!

Sometimes, as he had a powerful engine on his boat he would teach two at once.

For his 18th birthday I bought him a new (unused) limited company. He formed a Board of Directors of his friends. My idea was that both sons would learn to run a company.

I think I became Chairman but did not get involved very much. He held regular board meetings. At one it was moved and suggested that the company name should be changed to Phantom Balls Ltd.

Further board meetings resulted in totally hiring the Hammersmith Palais for a Saturday night and running a black-tie ball for youngsters.
One of the features was a mud wrestling area. The evening was a great success and finally broke about even – not bad for a new company.
I was sitting upstairs in the equivalent of the Royal Box when somebody asked me if the girl mud wresters could take their bikini tops off. Jolly good idea I replied.

My friend Tony was planning to spend 4 or 5 days on my boat and was looking out for a juicy book to take with him when he saw advertised a book titled 'how to hug'. The postage sounded expensive so he calculated that it must be quite a big book.
The book duly arrived, and he put it in his 'sailing bag' unwrapped to take with him to the boat.

It wasn't until he settled down in bed the first night when he unwrapped it and found to his horror that 'HOW TO HUG' was the 6th Volume of the Encyclopedia Britannica!
Whilst in Hythe, we heard the news that the American Aircraft

Carrier 'Forester' was moored off of the Isle of Wight. We thought it would be fun to sail out to her.

On arriving close by the Warship, we saw other yachts mooring up to a 'slipway'. The Carrier had lowered at the stern of the ship.

I am a qualified radio operator, so I called up 'Warship Forester' – this is how you address all 'Military' type ships, on radio channel 16. They asked me – as is correct procedure to switch to another channel which I did.

Unbelievably, as I requested permission to moor, the radio officer I was talking to replied – well we have just lost the Rider Cup – no you can't moor – 'Forester Out'.

If he had not heard about losing the golf we may have got on board for a coke.

We kept 'Uplands Lady', our 34-foot Moody which had sleeping for 6 in one large double cabin, 2 single beds in the front pointed area (called the bow) and the lounge can be re-arranged by dropping the table down to form 2 more beds, in Hythe, near Southampton during the Winter we kept her on our own pontoon just outside our house. In
April or May, we would sail her to Salcombe where we paid for a pontoon in 'The Bag'. We would bring her back in September or October – often in irritable seas.

During 1989 mobile phones were just coming in. I had one which was quite heavy and came in a leather case with a shoulder strap. The guts could be taken out and slotted into a unit in my car boot and another into a rack on board the boat. Whilst the office was working, the office could only phone me when we were in Salcombe for about 1 hour each side of high tide. At low tide I didn't have a signal. I always left my right-hand man who was a girl with Tide Tables – she was good at getting hold of us.

The other option was to use the radio telephone – I think the office found it quite amusing saying 'over' or 'out' after each sentence.

The office had a special number which got them through to BT's radio telephone system.

To use this system, I had to pass an operator exam in London especially learning the use of SOS.

You may be interested – SOS would be sent on channel 16 if the ship was actually on fire and/or sinking giving a real liability of death.

In an emergency just below this level one calls channel 16 and repeats "Salonce, Salonce".

In both cases one would then give the ship's name, position and type of emergency.

I and a friend are on board Uplands Lady in Salcombe when the following humorous, yet very sad situation occurred. A houseboat was moored in the "Bag" some 3 or 400 yards from us. This had a large flat roof with a safety 'fence' around the edge. Now people have just moved in and a few of them were dancing on the roof including one guy in a dark suit speedily walking up and down the length of the roof smoking a pipe – very odd, it was a fairly hot day.

Later in the afternoon we could just about hear a faint female voice quietly saying, "can somebody help me".

We jumped into our little grey blow-up boat and motored in the direction of the voice.

Wow! It took us to the houseboat and a woman waved us in to where there was a large guy who had fallen in the water and could not get out.

This looked dangerous. I was told that the houseboat had no life jackets or safety rings on board!.

I got down and held onto the guy in the water whilst my friend went back to our boat for the life vests and ropes.

We could see he was big and we were not going to just lift him out so the first job was to get a rope under his arms and tie him to the horizontal hand rails at roof level.

We could, with all our strength inch him up a little then tighten the ropes. Repeating these some 15 to 20 times we got him sitting on the deck of the houseboat. It was only then that the quietly spoken woman who raised the alarm said that she and her male partner were here giving a group of ESN patients a holiday.

Not a good idea.

I presented the woman with my emergency S.O.S. horn and insisted any more problems she must blow it to attract attention, and explained S.O.S.

I was concerned for all their safety.

1989

When I was promoted to Managing Director of C J Jefferies Ltd, my Chairman suggested we should apply for Quality Assurance BS5750. I had no idea what he was talking about but soon realised that this could put us a step ahead of our competitors.

Our head of Estimating and Transport Manager, John Cunnington (JC) would be the guy to deal with this. Some 6 months later we were awarded our QA Certificate.
I receive a letter from Debrett's asking if I realised I had an entry this year. I had given them information several months earlier.

Why am I listed? May be the publishers knew I would buy a copy for £57-50 which of course I did.

First job having become Managing Director was to go and see the Company Secretary and confiscate all of her foolscap and quarto paper – I had secretly risked ordering some A4 headed paper and presented her with a pack – that wouldn't last long but this procedure prevented an argument.

Now back to my Secretary – I was tempted to throw her typewriter away but I realised that this would not be the best way forward. IBM had just brought out their 'golf ball' typewriter and she was keen to get one. One arrived a day later.
Simple programming could be carried out I was told. For example,

all the words xxx could be changed to yyy by pressing a button (it became clear that it was more complicated than that).

About a week later a 200-page specification was ready to go out to tender and 10 copies would need to be printed and ready to go to the tenderers tomorrow.

The print run had begun when a phone call was received from British Telecom requesting a change in the type of tender.

There are many types of tender, but BT normally used one of two types:

"Domestic" where the company tendering can employ (within limits) any companies they like as sub-contractors for specialist services.

"Nominated" where the company tendering must use subcontractors specified by the Client.

In this case BT had required a Domestic type of contract and the tender was to be returned costed on this basis.

The phone call instructed that the contract and therefore the tender must be based on a nominated basis.
Easy with our new typewriter(s), just instruct the machine to change the word "Domestic" to "Nominated" throughout the document.

Oh dear, our domestic hot water, domestic cold water suddenly became nominated hot and cold water. We therefore had to go back to our older method of changing each page as necessary by hand.

New-fangled typewriters are not always the best!

AMERICA

I am on holiday for a few days in America and via a friend of Yvonne's managed to obtain a special pass signed by President Ronald Reagan to visit the White House on the 4th January at 8.30

a.m. Not many of these passes are issued – our Pass No. was 834. This gave us unprecedented access to areas not normally accessible to the public.

We (as most visitors do) became embarrassed when our guide said 'and then the British burned it down!'.

Through a similar route, I received the first (of many stages) invitation to the Inauguration of George Herbert Walker Bush as President of the United States of America on Friday the 28th January 1989. I didn't take this any further.

1990

I believe I officially joined the Conservative Party whilst living in Bisley in about 1990 although I used to get involved back in mid-1970's when the local doctor and me did a Punch and Judy show, Jubilee year.

We were getting more adventurous with the boat (called a yacht) visiting Guernsey, Jersey, Sark, France as well as most of the harbours on the South Coast.

One evening we were sitting in the back of the boat with our G&T's and wives (3 of us) when we saw a shining spot of light shoot across the sky – reverse and shoot back again. I said let's say nothing but go down to the chart table and write down what you saw. We all did this, and all notes agreed.

I would sometimes have staff from the office as crew and head for the pub at about 11.00 a.m. If I didn't think going for a sail was a good idea right now I suggest the candle test.

Just light the candle, hold it outside the door then bring it back in. If the flame is not blown out there is not enough wind to sail, if it blew out there was too much wind to sail comfortably. Later in the day I felt sure it would be o.k.

Sally, our Senior Manager in the office and a Director of Q.A. Services Ltd seemed to have incredible eye-sight – first class for the night watch when crossing the shipping lanes in the English Channel. I may see a ship's light, but she would know immediately if it was red, green or white.

At navigation classes, to pass the exam we had to be able to identify lights and other signs seen at sea. If we saw a red light – this meant the ship was passing across us from right to left. If green it was going from left to right.
We just steer for the back of the ship (stern). We should miss it then. If we saw a white light we were looking at the stern of the ship and it was going away from us. Some boats have special lights hanging in their mast to let us know the type of ship or boat it is.

For instance, two lights, one red and one white, one above the other (white at top) means it is a trawling fishing boat (these are just outlines – see Appendix for more information.

A fishing vessel that is NOT trawling displays red over white – to remember red over white frying tonight – a fishing boat.

During daylight hours the ships and boats hang shapes up in their mast. I will not bore you further.

You do have to know; if you are sailing into a marina or port and you see a green or red buoy or both, you must keep the green one on your right, if you don't you will wish you could swim better than you can.

Just to be awkward some places in the world have the buoys the other way round.

Check the almanac if you visit a Channel Island!
When in port at Salcombe, we hang a bucket up close to the top of the mast – this means we need water, and the water tanker will come to us and fill our tanks.

When we docked in Southampton at our house, and we know a large passenger ship was leaving such as QE2 we would position ourselves where we would not be a nuisance when QE2 moved down towards the sea – we would then enjoy escorting her out. This impressed Clients if I had them on board

We also enjoyed the band usually playing anchors-away as she slipped her birth.

Newcomers ask which side of the 'road' you drive when driving the 'Dorey' – this is a boat that takes us from the shore out to our yacht.

The full rules are complicated, but a good start is to drive, or pass on the right if convenient to do so. You can pass on the left, but you must make it VERY CLEAR to the other boat that that is what you intend to do.

You hear power gives way to sail well, if the boats are about the same size, this rule should be observed but if our yacht faces the QE2 it may be best for the sail to get out of the way. Likewise, swimmers have seniority!

I discovered roaming around with nothing on was a good feeling. I have also always liked a tanned body, so put the two together and I'm called a naturist.

I have since been on several naturist holidays, and as my garden is not overlooked often took my kit off – not many people know this!

Bottoms are the most difficult bit to get brown. Joyce fortunately is not inhibited! A standard joke is that when we go on organised naturist holidays we have 2 kg weight allowance on the plane. This covers shower bag and a towel!

If you have not tried this – give it a go all tensions and worries suddenly disappear when the last bit comes off! When on naturist holidays abroad you will notice that most guys keep their watches on, and they are nearly all VERY EXPENSIVE! – It seems to be a rich person's pursuit!

I recall chatting to 3 girls around the pool in Spain – I said I would love to see you girls in your clothes – a date was made for 6.30 in the bar – this is not the usual way round!

For those who have never been involved – there is one important rule in hotels or other public locations – YOU MUST SIT ON A TOWEL.

An important guy in Africa sued another for $10,000. (I will use non accurate figures to explain the point) and the Judge found in his favour. The Defendant stood up and said – 'Mr. Judge, yes I feel I owe Mr. Smith an apology so I would like to actually pay him $20,000 for his trouble.

Our guy realised there was clearly a reason for this, and it became clear that a cheque for $20,000 would bounce and the court case would have to start all over again. He cleverly found out how much the Defendant had in his bank account – let's say it was £15,000. Our guy paid £6,000 – the cheque for $20,000 was fast cleared and it did clear. Our guy made £20,000 - $6,000 = $14,000 - $4,000 more than he sued for! – all suggested by the Defendant and approved by the Judge.

We are staying on Uplands Lady, and it was Village Day – the day in the year when all the flags go up and most shops have a surprise bargain and 'find the mistake in the window to win a prize'.

On a yacht we keep about 40 flags to enable us to hoist various messages.

On special days we can 'overall dress' the ship by tying all the flags along a line from the stern (back) to the top of the mast and down the other side to the bow (front).

All the flags are given an alphabetical letter.

For instance, a red flag is 'B'. A yellow flag is 'Q'. A red and white flag is 'F' and a flag split into 4 parts, 2 red and 2 white is 'U'.

I'm not sure that I could be bothered to deal with tying all those flags up when a guy I knew asked if I would like him to overall dress the ship.

"Yes please".

We went to town for several hours. On our return all the flags were flying. Wonderful.

Sitting down now with a normal gin and tonic, I started reading the flags, the first was F, the second was U, wow – what's this about. He had signed "F*** the Club I'm off".

I asked Yvonne to take the flags down and jumped in the little grey boar and headed to town to find him.

I was told he had left the village having been sacked earlier that day. But, why my boat?

Hopefully not many people can read flag language these days!

1991

Sitting in a night club with some clients, about 9.00 pm, it occurred to me that if JC could get us the coveted QA Certificate, he could do it for other companies. I phoned JC, "can you get to London – got an idea" - "Yes ok".

I put it to him that we should form a company QA Services Ltd and offer your expertise to other companies. You will be the Managing Director. He suggested Sally should join us. Agreed. Buy 2 more cars tomorrow – one each.

Although the girls on the stage were naked we did not notice being excited with our ideas.

QA Services Ltd was to go on and obtain certificates for some important companies including parts of London Transport.

As previously mentioned, BPA was started in order to design a Hospital for Frankland International for final ownership by a major American Healthcare Group.

One hospital we got involved in was situated at Southampton and as we were asked to look carefully at infection control to a theatre dealing in the main with Orthopaedic work I looked into many aspects such as speed and direction of air flow over the operating table. (Existing rules simply say that Reynolds number should not exceed 18). The cleanliness of the air entering and blowing down onto the table was critical. The air filters were normally pink standard which is very high.

Off I went to Harwell Atomic Energy establishment realising that the filters used here must NEVER pass even pathogen size particles and not leak when they are changed.

I found a source of filter better than we currently used in operating theatres.

One problem was TM Regulations set out the type of filter to be used in theatres and I was actively going against the code if I specified my new find and could be in serious trouble and financially embarrassed if my filters failed the "certificate to operate test".
Well never mind about that – we specified the new type of filter. The day came for the test – petri dishes are placed round the theatre to see what bugs grow.

After 3 days the test was abandoned as no bugs grew so the petri dish gel must be at fault. The test was conducted twice more with just the minutest sign of a bug on the second one. The filters worked. We used these in all future theatres.

I felt TM's should be changed – it was, however, decided to leave the TM's as the minimum standard. By now filter manufacturers were marketing our find as theatre filters.

Jolly good.

In 1991 having moved into Vineyard Haven, a new house, and sorted out the house.

It was time to deal with the garden which had just been left as an area of clay.

I needed something to dig into this so off I set to a farm – could I buy a trailer of cow dung. Big discussions but in the end the farmer agreed, and a trailer load was delivered to the side of the house next to the kitchen door. I could smell the cow dung from the end of the road.

What I didn't know was that my wife Yvonne had a cooking club meeting that night – she was not happy with me.

1992

Very soon we had a pond, brick barbeque, green house, and workshop. I'm 50!
Let's have a party in August.
I approached a wine bar I frequented in Holborn to deal with the catering.

I had a telephone call from a Member of Parliament who I did not know asking if I could sit on a Committee who were to look at the future of photovoltaic cell use. Not to take part but to report on the usefulness of the Committee.

I was happy to do this even though there was no fee payable.

During the meeting somebody whispered in my ear requesting I see them prior to leaving.

A Member of Parliament saw me at the close of the meeting and asked me if I could help the people of Laos – what do they want? They require a network of refrigerators throughout the country, most of which has no power provision hence the probable use of solar voltaic cells (now known as solar panels) to power the refrigerators for the storage of 'prescription' drugs under the supervision of the 'local' physician or nurse.

I managed to obtain a free sample of a small solar panel, and a drug refrigerator and got it flown out F.O.C.

The Laos government were very pleased, and they arranged the wiring and installation.

Unfortunately, the panel and refrigerator were stolen a few months later which made us re-think the plan.

Laos was, and still is, a fascinating wonderful country, one feels very safe in the Capital City of Vientiane. The country was a Kingdom from 1946 until 1975 when it became a Democratic Republic.

I flew to Vientiane the Capital of Laos.

The population is 64% Buddhist and the Princess I got to know insisted I attend the local Temple, known as a Wat. On the way there we arranged for the driver to stop so that we could buy fruit at the roadside.

I was embarrassed when, on arriving at the Wat and seeing a very long queue to get in, and seeing the Princess all the people in the queue pushed us to the front. We paid a small amount of money for a small bird in a cage that we later gave its freedom.

I then found out what the queue was for. Just inside the Wat was a gold finished Buddha about 2'-0" high which you could try and lift.

If you, in your mind, wished for something, if it was, one day, to be granted then the Buddha would be light, and you could easily lift it. If there was something wrong with your wish the Buddha would be extremely heavy, and the strongest person could not lift it. I watched many try.

I can now reveal that I wished for success for my mission to Laos and I could not lift the Buddha – I asked if I could do it again asking the Princess – "yes of course". This time worded my wish a little different adding "eventually" – and the Buddha was extremely light as though made of thin plastic!

Truly amazing and emotional. We then went outside, gave our little birds there freedom after giving our fruit to the Monks.

I did some back of envelope calculations and came to the view that the Mekong River could support 2 or 3 more electric generating dams.

I flew to Vientiane again and met the Minister to the Prime Minister's office, Minister of Science, Governor of the Central Bank, and lots of other important people. I became a friend of the King's daughter, Princess Sunsumon.

They explained that what was really required by the population was a false leg facility today known as a prosthetic facility.

Knowing that the government control mineral deposits, gold mines and other sources of capital I thought something could be done.

It was not going to be effective to dive in with massive plans.

I arranged a series of meetings in London based upon times that the Prime Minister and his entourage could make but giving me 6 to 8 weeks to plan a sensible approach.

In the meantime, I contacted Roehampton Hospital who were very helpful and at a reasonable charge would be happy to fly out prosthetic fitting experts to train local personnel as soon as I had arranged the building.

BPA quickly designed a suitable facility working closely with Roehampton.

So, as soon as the London meetings were scheduled I could present the Prime Minister with a set of plans and schedules such that the facility would be opened in about 6 months' time – he was thrilled.

By now I was dealing with the World Bank and incredibly the Director, who would be responsible, I knew as he was a Director of a major London Bank who BPA worked for, providing air conditioning services to several of their buildings. He was content to cover the cost until an acceptable investment policy was agreed. Other disciplines were going to be required including investment specialist – world trading specialist – tree and forest management specialist if we were to expand beyond this facility.

I could see that the future London meetings were going to consist of 20 plus persons.

About this time my wife shouted up the stairs to get up as she had exciting news. Without my knowledge she had entered me in the worldwide 'lottery' to win a green card to allow one to work in America. I was unaware that she had become fond of an American guy who lived opposite, hence her wish to get to America.

"I had won"!
Winning the chance of obtaining a green card is only the beginning of a series of steps who I guess most people would not be able to follow – I had to get a job in America and confirmed by a Notary.

It was a good job that I used to work with a close friend and the two of us applied for a job in the USA. Just prior to going I was offered an Associate Partnership with my Company, doubling my salary – I stayed – he went, but could I track him down? One way would be guessing he would be a member of the American Society of Heating Air Conditioning and Refrigeration engineers – I was a member. I phone them "do you mean THE Mike Wren of M E Services" – well I might – and yes it was him and was able to make contact and obtain employment by amalgamating our two Companies. I became Vice President World. After medicals we obtained our green cards.

I was always looking for investments and my wife quizzed me on where property prices are rising most in the World. – Japan – no, London – No, elsewhere – answer – Virginia in USA. She suggested we should purchase a property there and rent it out to generate profit. Indeed, this could be done with a Mortgage to buy, such that the rental income would be more than the Mortgage. She then presented me with numerous pages of paper forming a Mortgage application form. I didn't like the endless questions and gave her a cheque for £85,000 to enable her to cash purchase. Much simpler.

I then found out that the house she had purchased was just round the corner from our American friend over the road's USA office and not far from his home.

We purchased the property in her name as that was to be preferred for tax purposes and furnished it – more money!

By now my wife and I were sleeping in separate bedrooms, but I always took her a cup of tea in the morning prior to going to work. One morning she was not in the room she normally slept in, nor was she in the blue room, orange room or the 5th room. I guessed she had gone off to work early. The two boys were at boarding school, so I had to just get on with my breakfast – what is this note next to the toaster? It read "left you, thanks for house, gone to live in Virginia"!

I went to work.

Now being employed in part in USA and married to my wife living in USA I had to complete the American tax return each year.

My wife (now ex-wife in practice) phoned to say her air conditioning would not work and the local store said a new system at about $20,000 was required – I knew this was not the case and she pleaded with me to fly over and help.

Time was tight in the office, and I jumped on Concord and arrived in 3 hours and took a capacitor out of the air conditioning unit (cost of a new one in UK about £3.00). As I had no idea where I could buy a replacement I suggested she phone the store who said the system requires replacing. A guy quickly arrived. I showed him the capacitor and suggested he could go and get one for me. I will happily pay $100. He was back in less than an hour with the unit. Thanks. I fitted it and all worked well, and I managed to get the Concord flight back.

Total cost $14,100, a saving of about $6,000. The big difference is I paid, not her!

C J Jefferies was for sale, and I proposed a possible management buyout – unfortunately the Chairman's brother who owned a shareholding wanted to sell for cash rather than shares in a much larger company.

The general plan was to form a group consisting of C J Jefferies, BPA, Wocad, R B Jefferies Ltd (a Maintenance Company), Jeffmet Engineering (a steel manufacturing company.

The Board would be formed from the existing MD's, and I proposed that my 'secretary' or right-hand man Sally would be Managing Director of the group and promote joint contracts.

Pete Marwick, our accountants warned that the plan to make Sally MD must be taken out of the business plan immediately – it looked as though there was more to this appointment than was the case 'sorry Sally' I have to take you out of the plan but as soon as things settle down you will be MD.

The entire plan did not come to fruition and Sally went her own way as a joint M.D. of Q.A. Services Ltd.
I should mention that Sally was a gifted manager of systems.

1993

A phone call requested we look into problems J P Morgan were having with their air conditioning. A briefing meeting will be held in the boardroom. I was one of the first to arrive and on the table was a message:

"Mr. Pitt please phone 0207 xxxxxxx ASAP.

So, I did and the guy the other end kept on about derivatives (I think). I didn't have a clue what he was talking about nor why he was talking to me. An hour later I was told that the Bank's Managing Director was Mr. Pitt!

Whilst the Senior Cabinet Ministers of Laos were here they were keen to see something of London, and Janice who looked after our money (I think she used to hide it in a cupboard) took them round including one Minister was keen to travel to Paris through the Euro Tunnel, whose services were designed by us.

One of Janice's customers who she would show round was in fact the Governor of the Bank of a large country.

After the visit, I flew to Vientiane and briefly addressed the Cabinet on a possible way forward – basically summing up the 1 week's visit to the United Kingdom.

We started planning ahead based on the necessary funding being confirmed. The Laos Government, at about the same time were looking to a planned future, and one alternative (of several) was to make me Governor of the Country together with some sort of tie with Britain. It was acknowledged that the European Union would be involved. Nevertheless, Janice and I were summoned to a meeting with them (who had been briefed by others) to agree salaries and some idea of procedure assuming we would both move to Vientiane. We agreed in principle.

Having lost everything – what do I do – well a friend who knew a friend lent me his narrow boat to stay on for a while, it was very cold with no heating.

I went to Dukes Wine bar where I knew the owner, John. He said he was moving, and I enquired who was moving into the cottage he lived in – nobody yet. Wow, I had heard he lived in a cottage on a Farm in Ottershaw – sounds just the job for me. He said he would introduce me to the owner.

I had just come from a meeting in London when he said come to the farm as the owner was available. I arrived in suit and tie and a Crombie overcoat with velvet collar – I think the owner, John, thought I was a stuffy accountant type – just the opposite to him who was a get your hands dirty worker. We really never got on.
Then, all my stored tools came out which impressed John and when he saw I could use them, we became close friends from then on until sadly he died from Leukemia in 2013. He was 1 day older than me. A fine feller

I should mention that John was quite a guy and when younger he got up to all sorts of mischief. His first "job" was mending up and down sliding sash windows especially renewing the ropes attached to the balancing weights.

He got most of his work by pulling on the ropes, letting the weight drop – this would break the old ropes – wow – of course the rope had to be repaired.

He tried his hand at being a coalman and ending up as a property developer!

John's wife, Pauline, now runs the farm and its 10 cottages and industrial units.

We have Paul on the farm who can take on any skill to the degree of a master. He is a master:

Plasterer Bricklayer Wood worker Cabinet maker Electrician Plumber
Underground drainage expert Painter and decorator Drives and roads

Any problems, call for Paul, he lives in Spain and travels here every 2 weeks to keep us all in good order.

1994

I wondered if I would have a uniform as Governor and would I live long enough to see the incredibly complex formalities through to a conclusion.

I received a phone call from my girlfriend Joyce – "Barry I need your help – a very good friend of mine has been beaten up by her fairly new partner and has turned up here for help but I have a house full of family. "Can you put her up" – "yes of course" - "I ought to tell you that she is black" she said (it turned out she was a beautiful bronze – just like I try to get on the beach. – OK simple, put her in a taxi and leave it all to me – she arrived with her daughter who was then 6 years old.
I had a spare bedroom – this is your room for as long as you need it. We became firm friends for the next 20 years.

She did, however, move out a few times then return having been beaten up again! One time she had a broken leg. Her room was always ready.

Living in a cottage on a farm she realised that there were empty stables and empty fields – "can I keep a horse here"? – I should explain that she was a horse nutter and expert rider.

I forget where the first horse came from, but I attended a horse auction with her and forgot to take my hand down and then realised I had bought a horse.

Barry's favourite horses were Olly, a very jumpy racehorse, and Cruse the friendliest horse ever.

Back at BPA and generally money problems were becoming important, we were not being paid as required by the Channel Tunnel Client – this was well known and often reported in the newspapers – so it wasn't just us, but that was no help. In fact, it got so bad the accounts guy and myself prepared a statement of affairs. Our Bank (Barclays) pushed strongly for us to settle the

£2,000,000 owing at 10p in the pound – well where were we going to find £200,000. No good going to our accountants for advice we were at war for refusing to switch us to a Limited Company some time earlier I was told the best answer was to be found by chatting to the girls and guys behind the counter at Guildford Court.

That's where we went next.

£2 million sounds a lot but some £1.5 million was owed on our houses which is payable over 20+ years as mortgages, but the total sums have to be considered when you calculate your position.

A lovely young lady behind the counter listened to our story – if you cannot get a loan to claim what you are owed by the Channel Tunnel you really are best going bankrupt. We looked at each other and knew this was really the only way to start sleeping of a night.

We asked her to make us an appointment for judgement. I said – is there a judge who could see us now – Oooh there may be – she picked up the phone and said 'Judge, could you see two nice men now'.

She said to go to Chamber No. 3.

We walked in – the Judge – no red gown or wig! – Made us welcome and we sat at a huge table – tell me your problems.

We explained – he said if you are sure, I can make you bankrupt now. Yes. He looked at his watch and said bankruptcy occurred at 10.55 a.m. We came out 2 feet talker and owed nothing to anybody except disappointingly to my son James, having lent me a £1.00 coin for parking.

I had lost everything, my home, my wife, all my companies but I was relatively happy.
I went into the office the next day – my bankruptcy allowed BPA to continue being managed by the Associates I had made, we made sure they had some money in the bank – but I could not touch it!

Looking back, I think the company would have performed better with just me as boss. The Associates only brought in minimum work yet were earning a lot of money.

As previously mentioned we had trouble getting the final account for the Channel Tunnel paid. I can't remember the outstanding debt but at one stage it stood at £150,000.

One of the problems was the computers that were going to be installed kept getting larger and larger giving out more and more heat. We totally re-designed the computer facilities 4 times, but our client claimed this was design development and not chargeable. They were wrong.

Work dropped off due partly to the general slowdown in the country.

I telephoned Pete Marwick, our accountants and said I wanted to go Limited.

They strongly recommended against this (in my opinion they were desperately wrong) as a lot of tax would become due. I was foretelling the future – bankrupting a limited company is MILES different to bankrupting a Partnership. I should have sacked Pete Marwick and brought in a more street wise accountant. Even today the large accountants are auditing massive firms who, surprise surprise go bankrupt just after their accounts are prepared!

1995

Having formed BPME, now an Anglo-American Company with me being appointed Vice President and Head of Operations worldwide including America, so now covering all areas of the World.

Time to think International and to this end we became part of an international team putting together many large projects.

Just a couple of amusing incidents came to mind, one was the provision of a Disco in Red Square, Moscow. Our team provided all services and unusually the facility required cooling when it was -30oC outside – all was finished on time with the exception of a bank of 'cubby-holes' to retain prohibited items for visiting clients. As these were not yet provided the Steward was given a cardboard box and some tie-on name tags.

Problem was the first to arrive were the first to leave and their property was now at the bottom of the box!

Yasser Arafat, the Leader of the Palestinians wanted a new Power Station and Airport. We agreed to carry out the initial design for the Benevolent Society of the Gaza Strip. As Mr. Arafat was in London it would be an idea to meet to see exactly what he wanted. Ken and I were to meet him on a Wednesday.

On arrival Ken went in to see him but I was not permitted – I didn't know why, so I shook hands with him with his office door open about 150 mm.

I told him anything agreed with Ken was agreed by me – fine and the door was shut. Ken came out about an hour later.
We then prepared what he wanted.

The Kingdom of Thailand State Railway required extensive extensions at about the same time.

A meeting was held including the highest level of management from the Bank of Thailand, the meeting was held over dinner in a Railway Station!

1996

Now BPA had amalgamated with ME Engineering (USA) to become BPME. We are moving into further international business.

I knew a guy I shall call Mr. East. He phoned me to say he was looking to take some upmarket offices in London and there is an area you could have if you are interested – well worth having a look.

Although he was the son of one of the richest men in the world (back then) he did not want to hold the lease – would I, if he signed a contract to pay £X per month for the term of the lease. Sounds ok.

It turned out that the office was in Charles Street just off of Piccadilly and my office window looked straight across the road to the entrance to Piccadilly Arcade.

An estate agent showed us round the offices, and it was agreed who would have what areas.

The agent said "we will repaint the ceiling where it is burned – oh how did it get burned?
Well, whilst filming Gold Finger the arc lights scorched the ceiling, the scene where a small guy throws his bowler hat at enormous speed in a posh office (mine). I said "No" don't paint it I like the story.

1998

Having completed a 7 ¼" (the distance between the rails) steam locomotive, it was about time I started building something else.

A 1/3 sized traction engine was the answer, and I purchased some pre-cut panels.

The side panels of the tender are curved and are stamped out by an enormous machine – I wanted a left- hand and right-hand panel. I bought them both together with some other parts such that I could make a start on the tender – the back where the coal is stored, and one stands to drive – in my case sit!

This is an unusual place to start but at that point in time I did not have a lathe, apparently the boiler would be 3 to 4 months delivery, so this was ordered. It was going to cost £1,200-00.

Between the boiler and tender are thick side plates called horn plates – it wasn't long before these were ordered and when the three pieces are riveted together one could see it was beginning to look like a traction engine but without wheels.

The wheels were next. Somebody else rolled the rims and fortunately laser steel cutting had been invented and the shaped spokes were cut by a company using this technique.

After about 5 years of work, I could light a fire under the boiler. After about an hour we had raised the water temperatures in the boiler and produced steam.

Into gear, open steam valve and off we went. Brilliant.

I had decided to build a 1/3 size traction engine. This means the model would be 4" for every 1 foot in the original full-size engine and is referred to as a 4" scale model. Off I went to D&S Steam Engineering Ltd, Northants to see a completed engine. They also sold the necessary castings and other heavy components.

The engine was finished in 2004 and named Winston (my middle name) and happily driven around the farm.

I then sold her with a view to building a larger one with 2 cylinders – Winston had one cylinder, and if she stopped at the wrong position of the piston, she would not start without a little push on the flywheel.

So, if there are 2 cylinders working 180º apart at least, one must be in a good position to start. WRONG. The high-pressure steam coming out of boiler does its work in one cylinder, and then, instead of being sent up the chimney, the steam still has sufficient pressure to work another cylinder – this second cylinder is called the low-pressure cylinder. So, if the first cylinder won't work due to stopping on or near Top Dead Centre (TDC) then 'no second-hand' steam will be going into the second cylinder. We therefore cheat and push a little button which gives a puff of high-pressure steam into the low (second) pressure cylinder and the whole lot starts 'Clever'

So, I decided to build a half size GARRETT Showman Engine.

A showman's engine is one with a long canopy extending to cover a dynamo in front of the chimney. These engines were the power houses for rides and lights at fairs. They themselves had lights all around the edge of the canopy – a fine sight.

If I wanted to use the engine in a public area, the boiler has to be made by a licensed welder and tested for leaks to 400 p.s.i. (pounds per square inch) if it is to normally operate to 200 p.s.i. all by a licensed Engineer. Delivery was going to be 1 year, and cost will be £3,000.00. A few points of interest to those just beginning to take an interest in Traction Engines follow. Alternatively jump a page or two.

The boiler (in this case 12" (300 mm) diameter and 3'-6" (1.1m) long. (The finished engine is 8'-6" (2.6m) long and 5'-6" (1.7m) high, the rear wheels are 3'-0" (0.9m) diameter in other words quite big.

Under one end of the boiler is a fire box which includes a grate on which we light a coal fire, pipes pass from the fire box to the front of the engine through which the hot smoke travels through from the fire to the chimney heating the water on its way which surrounds these tubes when the water gets to 100°C it starts to boil and generates steam – as the temperature goes up the pressure goes up as well until the pressure gets high enough to operate the safety valve(s).

High and lower-level tapping's on the end of the boiler are connected with lengths of glass tube enabling us to see the level of water in the boiler.

As the steam is used to drive the Engine the water level would go down.

We therefore have a tank of water under the driver's area and a pump that pumps water into the boiler. This pump is normally left running, and a valve is included to put the water into the boiler or back into the tank.

After the steam has pushed the piston up and down or in and out the used steam is sent up the chimney through a nozzle, this gives a blast up the chimney creating a draught which helps pull air through the fire. More air = more coal burning = more steam.

Damn clever really.

What would happen if I/you forgot to put more water in the boiler? Well, if it went almost dry it would get hotter and hotter and in the end, if the safety valve(s) were jammed the boiler would explode!

So, in the bottom of the boiler above the fire box is situated a 'fusible plug'. This is a plug with its centre made of lead. In the

end the lead would melt, and the remaining water would issue through this plug over the fire and assist in putting the fire out.
Also dam clever!

You may be interested to know my language gets a little blue whilst bending the wheel spokes to shape! Each one can take 3 or 4 goes before it fits nicely. If there are 2 or 3 at the wrong angle the wheel won't run true.

Riveting the spokes to the rims with 3/8" (10mm) diameter iron rivets is almost impossible with a hammer in a home workshop – I decide to cheat by threading the rivets and turning the nuts to look like round rivet heads with a minute flat to enable the nut to be tightened with a spanner, then the whole rivet and nut fixed with Araldite adhesive.

Speaking to a stress expert and also to my Engineer friend Dick, who helped to design the wings to the hurricane fighter plane. They both thought the spokes should be professionally riveted and not glued. The owner of the patterns for the castings and supplier of large components could power rivet them for me.
All the home-made rounded nuts and bolts came out (with much difficulty) and replaced with standard nuts and bolts and I made ready to deliver 4 wheels to Leicester – some 150 miles away for power riveting.

Solid rubber tyres can be vulcanised onto the wheels by specialist companies, and I had already booked them into a company in Yorkshire. So, in 2 weeks' time I collect 4, now riveted wheels from Leicester and with them in the back of the Land Rover drive on to Yorkshire. A total of 360 miles round trip.

I arranged for them, now with fantastic tyres, to be transported back to the farm at cost.

Brilliant, I am so lucky, on the farm there are craftsmen of all engineering disciplines.

Grant would always be willing to help when I was too scared to drill large holes by hand and is an expert at cutting plate and sheet steel.

Colm is a gifted guy when it comes to spray painting and is one of those that achieves a perfect finish – just what I need.

Not only that but he had just painted something in the exact shade of yellow colour I wanted for the wheels of my Showman Traction engine, and he had some paint left over! Free Paint – what more could you have – a world class painter and free paint!

The tyres are about 2" (50mm) thick solid rubber and I calculate they should be good for 3,142,000 miles provided no speeding.
Andy, my human crane, he was forever carrying the heavy cast iron cylinder block from bench to engine and back again many times. Carol, who has worked with me for some 30 years', is now typing this book – No Carol – no book!

1999

The landlord of an enormous block of flats in London had heard about new very efficient condensing boilers with 2" flues and had telephoned the boiler manufacturer, Keston Ltd, saying he wanted these to provide heating to "his" block of flats. The Managing Director of Keston Boilers suggested he contact Barry Pitt who may be able to help him. At the time these boilers were considered the most efficient in the world.

Here he was on the phone saying he wanted the boilers to replace the, what he thought were enormous oil-fired boilers in the basement boiler room. I had to tell him that the Keston condensing boilers were not really made for this purpose, but I would see what I could do. The result was a battery of 12 of his favourite boilers with their 2" flues discharging into a 20" diameter flue with a complicated system of fans to ensure each boiler was happy however many were firing, when I costed this the landlord and committee decided they could not afford it.

I visited site and found 3 cast iron boilers each rated at about 300 kW. I was able to give them 10 years' life. One broke down in the 11th year.
I ended up managing the services to this block of 50 upmarket flats, and as the residents committee assured me that the boilers would be replaced shortly I was to keep them going at minimum

cost. Now, in 2018 they have still not been replaced according to a friend who owns one of the flats.

I tried very hard to sell them renewable energy. The committee called a meeting of the residents for me to address.

I explained that with investment now, their heating and hot water would cost in the order of 60% less than it does now because right under where they were sitting and only about 18 metres down there was an underground river or an aquifer as it is more accurately known.

As the aquifer water was always a little warmer than our general surroundings we could take some water from it, subtract some warmth and put it back again slightly cooler in the winter and slightly warmer in the summer. Modern heat pump technology does the rest.

Sadly, this was far too advanced for most of those attending who thought that just changing to gas boilers would be a more reliable route.

Even in 2001 I stressed that they should seriously consider alternative energy as I predicted that the use of gas must be seriously reduced to meet global warming requirements. The result of this will, in my opinion, result in very heavy duty or tax becoming payable on all energy sources other than electricity as central electricity can be generated by tide, wind and other renewable sources which are not practical locally. Heat pumps are the way forward for the time being.

With this heat pump system, by flicking a switch the generation of heat can be changed to generating chilled water to give the flat owners almost free air conditioning once the necessary pipework had been installed and paid for.

2001

A letter arrived from a significant well-known Bank who had not paid their rent for 2 years due to the air conditioning not working.

Following a meeting with our Client, the Bank, who was now also suing the building owner. I quoted £100-00 per hour – plus payable if my endeavours won the Court Case a £10,000 bonus.

I found out that 3 or 4, and maybe more, companies and consultants had tried to solve the problem.

Half a day spent in the plant room gave me all the evidence I needed as to why it would not work to specification – it had been designed wrongly years ago when the plant was installed. The condenser was trying to work as an evaporator and the evaporator was trying to work as a condenser – it looked ok, but the compressor and expansion valve were also wrongly connected, effectively trying to run backward. I presented our barrister with my findings and the building owner's barrister accepted my explanation and the matter was settled just prior to going before the Judge.
The owner had the necessary work done and I was paid £11,100-00. Very satisfying for about 10 hours of work!

Two Partners, one being me, of BPA decided to sport £20.00 per month and buy penny shares, each taking it in turn to select what shares to purchase.
After 6 years we had spent £3,600 but our portfolio was not making reasonable money. It was my turn to choose – I suggested we sell the entire portfolio – some 70 items and later re-invest. Good idea my partner said.
Unfortunately, the City got to hear about this, and the result was devastating – the 2008 crash. I felt guilty and apologise to the World for causing this.

2006

I set out with Romany and Danni to look at a new horse. Unknown to Romany and Danni I took £500 cash with me.

On arriving at the stables, we noticed a good-looking thoroughbred horse in a field. The horse(s) we had come to see did not seem to be about. When the thoroughbred came over to the fence we were stunned to see she had a rope halter on with rope burns around her ears and what looked like a wound on her chest.

This horse was not in a very good condition. I said to the girls – we can't leave this horse in this guy's hands, let's try and buy her.

I offered £500 – this was accepted. We would have to get her into our trailer – I paid the money. All of a sudden, the horse disappeared.

Cutting a long story short the horse was now ours and the previous owner had stolen her

We phoned the police and reported a case of horse stealing – this is still a very serious crime.

I told the previous owner that the police were on their way – all of a sudden he disappeared and returned with the horse. We soon found out this could be a dangerous horse, but Romany and Danni were both expert horse handlers.

After quite a fight and much skin coming off my palm we got her into our trailer and took her home.

Her official name was Olympus and we got to know her as Olly.
We changed her official name to 'Uplands Lady', fully registered as a Bay Filly thoroughbred, born 2002.

You will find a photo of her jumping if you search your phone or computer for 'Thoroughbred Horse Uplands Lady. I took the photo!

Three different vets looked at her chest wound – none could heal it. Then Romany stuck pads of Hibi Scrub on her wound and she was soon all healed up. It clearly says on the bottle must not be used on infected wounds. Good job the horse couldn't read!

Her pedigree indicates some important parents and grandparents including a Grand National winner and Secretariat who was the fastest horse ever on our planet at that time.

One problem was nearly every time somebody got on her she would throw them off.

I spent a lot of money on her things such as one of the best saddles – especially fitted for her unusual, sloped back.

Yvonne's father suddenly felt ill when he answered the door to his sister who was visiting him.

An ambulance was called, and I went to the house as his sister may be left on her own – she was. I took her to hospital; we were shown to a side room close to A&E.

What looked like a senior nurse came in saying he arrived very ill – he was very ill when he arrived – he was found ill at home. What was this guy mumbling on about? I said – he has died hasn't he – Yes the nurse said with thanks that he didn't have to tell us. His sister went wild, running in circles and shouting no-no-no.

I caught hold of her to try and calm her. A policeman walked in – I asked him what he wanted. He explained that anybody who dies having been brought into A&E requires investigation. Nothing more happened.

As Arthur was in the RAF he was entitled to a Union Flag over his coffin. Oh dear, there is a special way of folding the union flag after use – phone J.C. – John can you fold the union flag (notice I am not calling it a Union Jack – it's called this only when flown on the stern of a Royal Navy Ship). No but I have an idea how it is done.

The next day I was able to calm his nerves (and mine) because the Funeral Directors would fold the flag. Some members of the local RAF Club turned up at the funeral.

2007

James my son, and his lovely fiancé decided to get married and started looking around for a suitable place to not only marry, but for the reception and all that goes with it.

He went to a Hotel/Club which I won't name and, I am told, the conversation went like this.

Fine, so how much is that wow, and we will require 3 or maybe 5 rooms – how much is that, and a cake is how much.

They were with a friend who added up all these figures and commented wow you could get married in Las Vegas for less than that I bet.

Good idea. To cut a long story short they got married in Caesars Palace, Las Vegas. This must be the ultimate venue and I understand cheaper than the club where they had enquired.

We were all booked into incredible suites and rooms in Caesars Palace.

After the Marriage breakfast some guests felt daring and took a ride rather like a roller coaster but 30 storeys above the road level. Very scary!
Happy Days.

2008

Need to sort out the Probate. Arthur's Will appointed a local solicitor as executor – I went with Yvonne to see them, wow they wanted £12,000 and thought it could take 6 to 9 months.

If all those included in the Will agree the executors can be changed.
Right, I offered to do the entire Probate and if I got it through Yvonne would pay me £4,000 saving her £8,000 - this was to be the bill for tooth implants I had planned. On receiving Probate and received a zero-tax demand. I phoned the dentist and made appointment for 4 implants.

Yvonne paid for 1 ½ then refused to pay the remainder. I have no idea why. I couldn't afford to have the work done and the result was one was half finished, one corroded at a later date (probably the wrong term) and had to come out. James, my son arranged an appointment with his dentist who unfortunately could not pull the thing out even with the greatest pressure and blood was going everywhere – the dentist had to go home to change his shirt. I was numb so no effect on me except his pushing and pulling.

I had to go to an Orthodontic Hospital to have it taken out. Eventually Yvonne paid a further £1,000 having previously paid £1,500. This covered my costs but did not give me the 4 new teeth I was hoping for; still she saved £9,500 yet still owed me £1,500.00.

The family were asked if there was anything in the house they wanted and after that the house would be cleared.

About 1995 Yvonne's Mother and Father moved into the house Yvonne was now selling. Realising they still had a high Mortgage percentage, and they were retired I offered to pay their Mortgage off in the sum of £40,000 then. As it was family there was no need to register this loan is there?

The house is now worth £300,000 plus. Being generous I suggested rather than me take the 80 odd percentage I put into it I will happily go half with you. No – I will make sure you get back the £40,000 you put in. Now Arthur left the two Grandsons and me £10,000 each. Yvonne's math's therefore calculated that I was owed £30,000 – which I eventually got.
I had to decide whether to demand half with the possibility of being at war for the rest of my life or remain friends and forego the £120,000 or thereabouts. I had no immediate use for a lot of money and decided to remain friends – which we have.

In this connection I was hoping for an insurance pay-out in 3- or 4-years' time as part of my main private pension became payable at age 70. I had held back about 20% of the pension pot to be paid to my wife on my death.

I had to name my wife and Prudential are claiming its payable to the name, the fact that she is no longer my wife is irrelevant. They now won't pay out when I am 70 as was agreed verbally with them years ago. Yvonne should get a few thousand when I die – I am, however, trying to put this off.

I was putting together managing methods for C J Jefferies Ltd. One of the first departments to be sorted out was tendering and costing. We had a new senior guy in charge of this department called John Cunnington. I learned much later that virtually all memos from the Managing Director (me) to him were quickly placed in the bin.

Yvonne and I had arranged a party at our Woking home and one of Yvonne's friends had just split up with her boyfriend – I was asked if there was a good-looking guy at work who could come with her.

I called Sally in (my female right-hand man) explaining I need a good-looking single guy to join one of Yvonne's friends at the party (that Sally had organised).

She said what about the new head of estimating, who embarrassingly I had not met.

Get him down here now.
She went upstairs and said to John – Mr. Pitt wants to see you in his office now.

I learned afterwards that he was convinced he was about to be sacked having put all my ideas in the bin.

It seemed to be ages until he arrived and looked positively miserable – I said – sit down – what are you doing Saturday evening? Nothing – good, come to a party at my place – don't bring a bird I've got one for you! He suddenly looked 3" taller and a giant smile arrived on his face.

2009

Returning to Olly our horse, I thought it would be a good idea and financially sensible to get her pregnant.

We looked at many stallions (boy horses). It was quite exciting and scary being close to relatively famous horses and discussing buying horse's semen. We agreed Kayf Tara would make Olly a good Husband and agreed a good price of £5,500 (from memory).

We had already arranged for a top vet (as used by the Queen) to check Olly out – she was A1 fit.

The vet was also going to arrange the artificial insemination which would include a 3 or 4 day stay at the vet's stables.

It was absolutely essential that Olly had a stress-free period of a month or so after coming home.

The day after she came home I found the owner of a woodworking company was driving a tractor around her field towing a topper. I signaled to him to stop but he ignored me. Olly lost her pregnancy.

This man cost me over £7,000. Not only that, as the field had not been used for about 2 weeks ragwort had not been cleared and could now be spread throughout the area. Not important but the rule is NEVER cut the grass in a field without checking with the user – I was paying for the use of the field and this guy considered this irrelevant.

I purchased more semen – it was put on a plane in Belgium. The airport was closed down and our semen became of no use – another £2,000 gone.

We gave up the idea of a baby horse.

As a fellow of the Chartered Institute of Building Services Engineers I take an interest in energy use and environmental pollution including global warming.

It is quite amazing that our building regulations do very little to reduce energy use and selection of fuel type.
2010

As far as the insulation of houses is concerned, we have a series of Codes, Numbers 3, 4 being most popular. Code 4 gives requirements which are now normally worked to giving better results than our building regulation – why are our building regulations always behind general thinking?

I mentioned to an owner of one of the flats in the London block I was looking after that I was (many many years ago) chairman of Bisley Conservations.
Oooh do you want to join up again, Foxhills clearly needs a new

Chairman.

A small meeting was arranged, and I was proclaimed Deputy Chairman. Would I stand as a candidate at the next local elections, 27th May 2014 – "Yes".

I won and having more votes than the existing independent, my win was celebrated as a Conservative gain.

During the year before the untimely death of the Conservative Councillor for Foxhills occurred which generated a by-election, there was little publicity and unfortunately many roads were not canvassed. ~The result was UKIP gained the seat totally unexpected.

I took an interest in planning and was placed on the Planning Committee. Two weeks later I was sacked and taken off this Committee, due, I was told that a longer termed person had been forgotten. This was strange as I had been told that another Councillor had been put on the Planning Committee but did not want this position.

I was reinstated.
The Town was going to redevelop an area of the Main Road with large shops, a cinema, and homes.
As an energy engineer and a Fellow of the Controlling Institute I was interested to see how the planning was going.

I was shocked to hear that the shops, flats, cinemas etc. were to be fed with heating water from a small, combined heat and power system and boiler.

I wrote to the Chief Executive asking why this doubtful arrangement was being installed instead if the latest technology of heat pumps such that very cheap cooling could be supplied in summer.

See Appendix why combined heat and power (CH&P) is not a good idea but suffice to say here that in the USA some states have made the installation of these systems larger than 10 kW, illegal due to their very low greenness!

I was issued with a copy of the document setting out the selection of energy equipment. It is about 20 mm thick and the first 50% of this document was recommending heat pumps, then for no reason I can see heat pumps are no longer being considered – only mentioned here and there.

Asking Officers why this sudden change over to CH&P, I was given to understand that this was a change requested by the Planning Department – whether it was Officers or Committee is unknown.

It was unlikely that shop owners would be interested in a development with no cheap cooling available.

The system proposed will result in between 300,000 and 600,000 tonnes of Carbon Dioxide per year, not including the homes, being generated from our site. If heat pumps had been proposed the total Carbon Dioxide from the site would be zero or close to zero.

The generation of CO_2 became the problem of central generation – this is going down as more and more renewable technology is being incorporated.

I also pointed out that in 20 or 30 years it is most likely that even flats will be requiring cooling resulting in hundreds of boxes screwed on walls all over the development.

Personally, I found the development miserable, no wow or sexy input at all. All the buildings are of a square nature.

In 30 years', time our site may be one of the un-greenest.

I think I have it round the right way – if a horse is free to turn his head, if he/she looks at you with his/her right eye he/she likes you. The left eye says he/she is questioning what you are like! If you are frightened of horses – and I don't blame you – they are ever so big and very strong.

You need to know it's not a good idea to walk closely or around the back of a horse unless he/she knows you are there.

If the horse has a nice red bow tied around its tail it does not mean it's going to a party. Actually, it's the international sign that the horse is known to kick. I would suggest you keep 1 field length away!

If you can't catch the horse you want to ride – best give up and get a horsey person to do it.

Our Olly would come nicely to us when we called her – I think because she was looking forward to throwing one off if you managed to climb onto her.

If you would like to know, best to get a book on horse riding.

If you do get on and stay on for a while just VERY gently "kick" with your heels of both feet whilst talking to him/her. Normal language for horses in Britain is English and most common command is "WALK ON" – you will be amazed he or she will walk straight ahead – you could steer by puling gently on the right-hand reign if you want to go to the right.

Best brake for a beginner is to pull VERY gently on both reigns and say Whoa.

Where I have said 'gently' made sure you do – change this word to 'strongly' you will set off on a 30-mph gallop and won't be able to stop. A better idea all round is to get a nice book.

2011ish

Antony, my son, buys me tickets for 2 to sail to New York on the new Queen Mary 2 – who will you take with you? – Joyce of course.

It was a memorable occasion. It would be easy to double one's weight on this trip with the tons of gourmet food available.

We all got up early to see us pass the famous Statue of Liberty but sadly it was thick fog, and we could not see the Statue. One older lady was almost uncontrollable at not being able to see it. There was also an enormous crane opposite our ship. I told her I thought that was the Statue but in the fog you couldn't really see it.

She was enormously grateful that I was able to point out the Statue and said how silly she was looking in the wrong direction!

Antony collected us at the Port, we took a taxi to the airport, flew to Los Angeles Airport where he had left his car to take us to his home. After a few days on his beach, we flew back to Heathrow and finally home.

2012

How can you best spend £2.00 per year, Answer – join the Local Residents Association and get a jolly good read twice a year and their Committee consists of persons who are all fonts of knowledge.

After becoming a Councillor this Committee often knew more than me on some important issues. As their Councillor, I commenced 'popping in' to their meetings and suggested a 'Councillor's Corner' in their magazine – this has become a regular feature.

A few of my articles will be found in my next book.

It's getting colder and Romany suggests Olly needs a coat put on each evening. I knew the horse could be dangerous and didn't want to put her coat on whilst she was in the field.

Romany said I would be quite safe and there was nothing to worry about. For some silly reason I did what she said but decided to give her some nice dinner that she could eat whilst I threw the coat over her. The coat was quite heavy. Once you have the horse's coat roughly positioned you have to be brave and reach under her tummy for the strap hanging down on the opposite side to you, bring it across and 'buckle it up' with the buckle hanging your side but at an angle. There are 2 straps under her belly, and they cross in the middle, i.e. left nearside goes to right offside, left offside goes to right nearside. You then clip her collar under her neck and her tail flap at her rear.

I never got used to this and was always nervous. In the coldest weather she would have two coats on, one on top of the other.

2013

The only time I have been on television was at the Surrey County Show when a pig escaped from the exhibition/judging area, and I (stupidly) stood fast to stop it. Woo. It was caught on television I was told but I didn't see it.

Now I'm 70 I am proud that I have all my own teeth, which does surprise some people who know my age. Some, however, were paid for by my sons but they said that I can call them my own.

2014

Now I was a Councillor I, and a very Senior Councillor attended WARA (West Addlestone Residents Association). My friend didn't live in the catchment area, but I did and joined. It was quite expensive £2-00 per year (what can you get for 3.8 pence per week). Sadly, I have since learnt that due to the lack of interest as far as Committee Members and Authors are concerned I have to report that WARA was wound up in May 2019. I must add my own thanks to the Committee Members, Chairman and Authors who served the community via WARA for some 52 years.

To become a candidate for Council I went before a Committee – passed, arranged for some literature to be printed and, come May, David a senior member of the Conservative Party arranges via his friends to get them through as many letter boxes as possible of the 2000 householders.

I then went round virtually all the houses, knocking on all of the doors. If they were not in I would leave a slip of paper saying 'called today – sorry I missed you'. Some people are amusing when they come to the door – although I wore a huge blue rosette they would want to know who I was.

Some said they were very cross with the Conservatives or the Government. I told them exactly what they should do if they felt cross "find my name on the slip of paper in the polling booth and put a good heavy cross next to it. You must let me, and others know you are cross, and this is the way to do it".

Some would come to the door and say they haven't decided yet – I would ask if they minded if I stood under that tree whilst you make up your mind.

Some Conservatives had red flowers in the garden – this is, I believe purely to confuse me.

On the day of the election, I would stand outside the polling station. The law is quite strict on what you can do here:

You cannot put even one foot inside except just once to cast your own vote or report a problem.
You cannot discuss any political matters within hearing distance of the polling station.
You cannot ask those attending to vote who they are voting for.
There are others.

What you do is ask them for their number where they are registered on the electoral roll.

I recall asking an attractive black girl for her number (which is printed on the card). They were sent out by the Council. Oooh yes she said of course …. 07836 192xxx.

Did she want me to telephone her?

I guessed not and didn't write it down

Previously, due to the death of a Councillor there was a by-election.

Two weeks before polling day the Prime Minister stated that same sex marriages were now legally ok.
95% of the residents in my area did not like this and took it out on me – many saying so as they went into vote. UKIP go it. A sad day.

I have now been semi-retired about 10 years, but old pals still phone me to see if I could help them. I only said yes if it sounded exciting. One such call was to survey a jet fighter airfield and base.

Yes.

The building we had to check out was between two runways – how do I get across these – rrr traffic lights and they were green SO GO.

Wrong it doesn't say so, but one has to get verbal permission AS WELL to cross on our way back, we were given a good talking to. Full marks to whomever the RAF got to look after the Mechanical and Electrical Services. We were to comment on alterations that were required.

During my period as a Councillor, I was quite astonished as to how the Senior Members and especially Head of Planning and Planning Committee treated Travellers and Gypsies as far as site provision is/was concerned. Site provision was always an afterthought. On one particular occasion an ideal site came up. I spoke for the planning (the site was owned by the Gypsy fraternity). Most of the other Committee Members said no but finally agreed to yes after a 5-year term was suggested. So, after 5 years they all get thrown out!

Still, if Head of Planning says xxx then 90% of the Members will say xxx there was only 3 or 4 of us who would argue when we were sure Head of Planning was wrong!

My cousin Mary's husband is Wally. If you used one of the top hotels in London you will have seen Wally in his immaculate brown suit as doorman to greet those going in as well as helping in every direction.

At a family dinner party, Wally left the table to go upstairs. Sadly, he fell and ended up unconscious against a wall at the foot of the stairs. Oh, my goodness, he was not breathing so I started CPR, one two three four, one two three four. I kept this up for a full 20 minutes when the ambulance arrived with paramedics. They took over. If you have never done this, believe me I was totally exhausted and could barely stand. Wally was alive when they got him into an ambulance.

Sadly, he died the following day in hospital.

He will be greatly missed – he always had a story to tell and was a wonderful guy.

2015

Each evening I put Cruzi away into his stable and in the colder weather put his coat on. As he was laminetic he could not eat grass, but I would give him two nice meals per day.

One evening, bringing him out of the field somebody had put a load of hard core by the gate but not rolled it flat. As we were both negotiating this someone started a motorbike which made us both jump, and I caught my foot between two or more bricks and twisted it – for some reason this caused a great pain in the calf.

Three mornings later I woke with a stone-cold left foot – this isn't right, after a shower I went to A&E.

The consultant who saw me put me on a drip – will I have to stay in tonight – yes could be for a week. I have a blocked artery in my leg and a dodgy aorta (the bottom half).

After many tests a vascular surgeon said we have two options:
Amputate your left leg just below the knee or try and deal with the blockage and be limited to 30 paces for the rest of your life

I chose No. 2 but would go along with whatever the surgeon thought best. No. 2 was the agreed way forward, operation took place.
18 months later I had a blockage in my other (right) leg. This was easier to deal with and I was able to watch the surgeon hook the blockage out with a piece of wire!

At the age of 18 as part of my apprenticeship I was working on a site in Romford. The laggers (insulation fitters) were mixing asbestos powder with water and some other additive to make a plastic like consistency to plaster onto the pipework as insulation. A very pleasant smooth plaster finished the job.
The air in the mixing areas was thick with asbestos powder.

This now manifests itself with hardening of one lung and other diseases with complicated names. 25% of one lung is collapsed.

In 2018 I needed another operation to sort out problems with some stents (short lengths of pipes put into or actually outside arteries where the pipes have weakened.

I recall that Yvonne's father died when his aorta burst in the same way as Carol's mother. This is known as Abdominal Aorta Aneurism or AAA.

I attended hospital for pre-meds.
The final decision was that I could not be put to sleep due to my lung condition and would have to have the operation awake. I did not know how long the operation would take – 3 years ago it took 3 hours

Oh well there we are.

I was shown into the operating theatre and climbed onto the operating table. A nurse tied my legs and arms down using sheets and a blue hood was placed over my head. This was not particularly nice.

I assumed I would be given a sedative by mouth, but it must have been injected because the operation commenced. All of a sudden there is a great pain as the surgeon worked – I shouted out words stronger than ouch, why can't I have an epidural, I was wriggling due to this intense pain – please give me more local anaesthetic – NO SHUT UP BARRY the surgeon shouted at me.

I laid very still and quiet after this even though the pain was perhaps level 8. BUT THIS SAVED MY LIFE.
I learned later that I could have bled to death if the surgeon could not stop a problem bleed and he could not deal with it whilst I was wreathing around.

I had had a maximum of several numbing drugs and could not have any more. The operation was taking longer than planned due to the surgeon having to cut through lots of scar tissue formed after earlier operations.

I sent the Surgeon – Mr. Ali a Christmas card writing inside

"THANK YOU FOR KEEPING ME ALIVE". I guess he got it.

To all building hydraulic engineers (sometimes called plumbers), I used to look after a block of some 50 flats over 6 storeys near Paddington. Being on site and having 2 hours between meetings I spent the time thinking about the problem Bob the Services Manager had every time he filled up this old 1933 heating system. The heating water used to be circulated around the radiator system by gravity in 4" pipes.

Around 1955/60 pump manufacturers were knocking on the doors of large buildings explaining the benefit of installing circulating pumps.

Many building owners had pumps installed to boost circulation with very limited, if any, calculation as to size or power of the pump.

It could take Bob best part of a week to clear the air from the radiators especially on the 6th floor. Now these pumps (as all pumps) suck water in one 'side' and blow it out of the other. If the system was a simple loop, the pressure in the pipe forming the loop would be positive about halfway and negative the other half back to the pump inlet. Perhaps about halfway the pressure would be 0.

If the radiators hitched into this loop are all on the 'negative side', opening the radiator vent valve would cause air to be sucked in, not water squirted out.

So, we want to move this zero-point to be situated after the last radiator on the highest floors around the loop. Now, these types of pumps work if running forward or backward. I won't bore you with the details, but I decided the 1950/60 pumps sizing was over the top.

The answer was to reverse the pump (just switch 2 wires round but do not do this unless qualified to do so).

The pump was left running backwards with no noticeable effect on the heating system.

A few months later the system had to be emptied, and on re-filling

Bob was delighted to vent all the radiators in no time at all!

We had a happy Bob.

I was then sacked as the building's consultant; the managing agent's services lady heard that I would be signing off invoices. Not a good idea she thought and said I was not required!

I wasn't too concerned.

She ordered a report on the Boiler Plant from one of her contractor friends – guess what – they found a pump running backwards and put this 'right' immediately.

Guess again, Bob could not fill the system.

Her contractor friend explained to the Building Owners that a pressurising set was required as the only answer instead of phoning me.

Some £5 or £6,000 I guess was spent installing a pressurising system.

Now installing a pressure set next to 70- or 75-year cast iron boilers which is in appalling condition is not a good idea. Strangely just after, boiler No. 1's crack got worse.

I am now a member of the Basingstoke Canal Joint Management Committee, where, as representing Runnymede Borough Council I was not too popular. Although Runnymede regularly paid their share of the maintenance costs, it was not the amount originally promised. I said at the public meeting I would see what I could do to increase the annual payment. Senior Councillors thought that the amount we were paying was fine.

2016

Now I have been a Councillor for 2 years and have learned the ways and procedures. One or two interesting matters came to my attention.
Four or five years ago it was decided to purchase several school

busses. I am informed that quotes were obtained from several coach dealers.

None of them could supply a coach that looked as most people pictures a school bus, which was normally based on the yellow American school bus with "SCHOOL BUS" over the front windscreen.

They decided to find out the cost of importing the real American school bus. It worked out the cheapest quote!

They were ordered from America. A team of drivers was dispatched to the docks to drive them back to Runnymede as soon as they cleared customs. Oh dear.

The buses could not get round the first roundabout without some 3-point turn manoeuvres!

There are almost zero roundabouts in America and the steering gear did not have to manage sharp turns.

All the steering gear had to be changed which brought the total cost up to the best British cost.

2017

The Basingstoke Council are purchasing a new narrow boat and guess what us members were invited to the new boat's initial trip. Wonderful, I and Danni decided to go. There was a bar on board and very good company.

Bang!

We had hit something sticking out from the shore under water. Several passengers fell off their chairs, but nobody seemed too concerned.

A wonderful evening, I can strongly recommend taking this trip it's only a few pounds. At Christmas the Santa Cruise costs about £14.50 per person. They say there is a slim chance of seeing Rudolph grazing on the tow path.

Or you can hire a canoe at £11.50 per hour.

Not many people know that a couple of crayfish got into the canal many years ago and bred to the extent of becoming a serious nuisance.

During the Summer of 2016, 7.0 tons of cray fish were removed by professional fishermen!

I was waiting in Tesco's to reach in to get a large carton of milk – the lady in front of me didn't know – I thought I was there – she was shuffling the cartons around – when she saw me she said – oh I'm so sorry I'm looking for a good date. I said 'I'm so sorry I'm busy tonight so I can't help – Oooh she said, I must tell my daughter!

Every 6 months I attend hospital for a scan to check up on the stents fitted several years ago to prevent my aorta bursting.

I've often considered this as my Father-in-Law and secretaries Mother both died due to aorta bursts.

The scan showed some problems and following a consultation with 'my' vascular surgeon – I say my because – Mr. Ali had operated on me previously. It was decided that he would operate; technically he would perform an endovascular aneurysm repair and angioplasty on one (or two) iliac arteries.

As I mentioned, the anaesthetist was not happy to put me to sleep for this operation due to the poor condition of my lungs resulting from having asbestos pollution at the age of 20, resulting in hardening of part of one lung and collapse of another part.

No problem – I confirmed I'll have it done awake assuming your local anaesthetic works – perhaps I could watch the operation on T.V. – "no you can't", came the order.

Quite happy with this but something told me it was going to go wrong – no idea why – I'm not a wimp. However, I found myself filling my personal box with things that would be useful to my sons should I die! – where to sell my traction engine and other similar stuff.

I chose the music I wanted at my funeral – why was I doing this? – I did not know but thought I should.
I selected 'Time to Say Goodbye' by Andrea Bocelli and Sarah Brightman – I was playing it excessively.

I've built numerous operating theatres as an Engineer and been in them during an operation a couple of times.

Walking into the theatre and climbing onto the operating table I felt uncomfortable – why? – I don't know why but there was something odd. My arms were then tied down – not with straps as it may have been many years ago but with beautiful silky sheets – but I was tied down and was not too keen on it.

A blue hood was then put over my head and an oxygen pipe leaked a little O2 for me.

Effectively I was tied down and blindfolded.

The blue cover was adjusted and as it was moved I could see Mr. Ali in his very colourful apron – he was painting me with a brown liquid – I guess iodine, but I don't know.

I was wrongly expecting to be given a squirt of sedative in my mouth, but this didn't happen. I do hope they are injecting it – I seemed to worry about everything – not my way – why was this?

As I mentioned, all of a sudden a searing pain in my lower side – I moved the best I could and started moaning with continual pain I shouted 'give me an epidural quick. The surgeon shouted back 'shut-up Barry' – this made me keep still even though the pain was extreme. I learned later that his shouting saved my life – don't wake up during an operation!

A T.V. programme showed this operation and explained that a percentage of patients bleed to death as the particular bleeding is incredibly difficult to stop. Mr. Ali stopped it while I was awake.

I think the pain caused a shock to the system. I think 2 days later my son came to pick me up – I wasn't feeling well but I had to get out of the Hospital ASAP. Next day I could not stop shaking and I was taken back to A&E.

If the guy in the next bed does not answer his phone soon – as ill as I feel I will go and hit him. Good job I didn't, the sound was from my heart monitor! They thought I may be subject to sepsis. I was put on antibiotics and sent to the ward.

I seemed to get worse. The head nurse moved my bed from the end of the word to opposite the Nurses Station – I'm thinking *(I don't know why it's me). This is where you are placed if you may die!

Danni comes to see me but didn't stay long – later she explained that I had that death look and didn't like it.

They guessed I had an infection – either lungs or urinal – they wanted desperately for a water sample, but I couldn't go – Antony was with me and quite rightly left – I phoned him on the way home – peed – well done Dad. Later that evening my blood pressure was very low and the intensive care team were called in.

It went even lower, and a doctor ordered that I must be ex-rayed and CAT scanned urgently.

11.00 p.m. – I am pushed at a great speed to the scan and x-ray department. I am put on 'exotic drugs' by drip for sepsis.

I swelled up all over my body and felt ill.

In 2 or 3 days I felt fine – no need for my music choice!

As a grumpy old man, I have moaned and groaned about the preparation of the 35-year plan being prepared by the Council Planning Department. The sections I have read are not aligned to requirements in my book and are pointing to failure, very bad planning!

The entire local population has been pushing for roads and infrastructure plans to be stated as required for the proposed housing, but Council Officers do not listen. The proposed requirement for housing is basically wrong with sites of cheap houses being tucked into any site including up-market areas, whereas there are areas of land that could be made available with almost no effect on neighbours.

Energy saving is barely touched upon.
In 35 years', time our way of living, bearing in mind we will have no gas for house heating, will be entirely different – such climatic changes have not been considered as far as I can see by 'Planning and our Council'.

2018

Brexit? Well, my view is very simple it may be more comfortable to stay in the fraudulent EU (they have never signed off their accounts and their CEO admits he tells lies) but one should remember just over 90,000,000 people were killed to ensure we were not controlled by the Germans in 2 World Wars.

Now some 50% of the population find this irrelevant and are voting in favour of being controlled by the Germans; incredible!

This can't be right. Other than Germany and Britain, European Union members have money worries but can't de-value or otherwise deal with their problems because the EU says so – not my idea of a happy future.

Why do we need a deal anyway? Trucks don't have to stop long now, why will they when we are free.

I have written to the Chancellor of the Exchequer who I know, clearly stating my opinion, which is not in agreement with his.

"Dear Chancellor

The EU will never let us totally leave and we will have very little say. Only other option is to leave with no deal and 20 minutes or less after leaving present the EU with a deal simply saying generally zero tariffs and carry on as we are". Some goods will have to have tariffs, but we have had 2 years to sort them out.

Although I know my email cut straight to two offices, I do not expect in these very busy times to receive a reply.

I have to say I do not like Prime Minister May. When she was Home Secretary, she picked on Black people by not letting them back in the Country when they went on holiday, stopped stop and search for knives, says we can't have a Boarder between North and South Island (when we already have one) if we do the locals will shoot each other – rubbish.

By the time you read this book you may know what happened. There has been no negotiation – what percentage of the 500+ page agreement was written by May's team – I have the answer, 0%.

Apparently, if one loses an election or referendum, you can do it again and again until you get the answer you want.

I assume then, we can re-run the last general election and fill the House with members who have higher IQ's than the present members. I listened to numerous speeches, not one suggested how to deal with the Irish Border problem – unbelievable.

2019

The "Irish problem" is manufactured by those in love with the E.U.

The existing border between North and South is signed by means of a small notice on a pole by the side of the road.

Percentage VAT is different on both sides – no problem you don't have to stop so different tariffs each side – ditto – don't stop. The correct tariff being certified at final delivery locations? – Answer isn't it!

I receive a letter from the National Health Service, actually from the Department of Urology. What for?

Unfortunately, the letter arrived the day after the appointment date referred to in the letter. I obviously missed the appointment. A further appointment was made by telephone.

Apparently, my Vascular Surgeon was looking at a scan to decide on some pipework required when he noticed a lump on a kidney.

Hence, he notified the Urology Department.

I went to see the Consultant Urological Surgeon who after checking the same scan, and one from a year before, he was fairly certain the lump was a cancerous renal lesion.
Pointing to an examination 'couch' in his room I said – well, have to come out – I'll lay down there and you go and find a scalpel. He said he wished it was so easy, but it would be an 8-hour operation which my body would not like. So may be better to just leave it as there is only a 1% risk of spread over a 3- or 4-year period, probably indicating a 10% risk over 10 years.

10 years! – brilliant, although the witch Doctor in Zulu-land said I would live to over 100.

I didn't like to say that the Senior Consultant was obviously wrong!

Looking back Yvonne, my ex-wife, thinks in my total of 49 years of work I was only off work 4 times, each time being about 1 week, all due to my 'bad back'. Not too bad a record. I was never off work due to colds and flu which everyone else seemed to get.

I have always been a firm believer in washing my hands frequently especially after meeting people and shaking hands. I also drank gallons of red wine!

One year I looked back and plotted when my back caused trouble.
*I also plotted when we first sailed our boat from Hythe to Salcombe.
There was, it appeared a connection, my back usually caused trouble 3 to 4 weeks after this trip and 3 weeks after the first time in the year that I threw the 30kg anchor over the bow.

The throwing, including lifting it above the safety rail and leaning out with it almost at arm's length to miss the hull when thrown, clearly an enormous strain on my back – but no effect at the time of throwing!

That must be my bad back cause.

I then had an electric anchor winch fitted. Lovely.

I attend a Conservative Executive meeting just before us members vote between Jeremy Hunt and Boris Johnson to become our leader and hence our new Prime Minister, as well as the unknown future as far as a possible General Election is concerned and this matter is not on the Agenda, and I am informed that there is no any other business.

The Chairman was not very happy with me insisting on bringing up the difficulty in obtaining membership cards.

I especially wanted to let all members know what I was told on the telephone from Conservative H.Q.
Dolsey, who was last year's Mayor chopped in saying she had the same difficulty.

I was told vote for leader was a postal vote – in other words shut-up.

Nevertheless, I was hoping to explain that if we had a sudden requirement to vote to select our MP we would not be required to show a membership card, but all those entering would be checked by entering their name into a computer – all, say, 200 of them!

There would be nothing to stop a, say, Labour supporter entering just by giving a known Conservative name.

The Chairman did not want to consider this.

31st December 2019, a strange case of an unusual type of pneumonia is found in China. This is caused by an unknown virus. It seems strange to me that it was in Wuhan, China just down the road from a virus laboratory.

UK to leave the European Union on 29th March but is delayed – this is the subject of another book!
May be this has all been considered and dealt with.

2020

World Health Organisation warns the World that the newly found virus could be of international concern. Nature, in my book, does not deal in viruses of concern and I suspect it was man-made, perhaps as a "chemical weapon" to be sprinkled over an enemy but it escaped.

A vaccine was made in a few days but had to be re-made slowly to comply with regulations. This is the stuff of another book!

I don't like the dentists, but I like walking passed the shop. Christina, who gave me the cover hammer for my birthday, worked there, so would pop out as I went passed, and for some reason I've never worked out would give me a big hug there and then in public.

Christina is the only good thing about the dentists!

2021

My cleaning lady decides to take up decorating, so I'm introduced to Claudia who lives on the farm and is looking for cleaning jobs. She becomes my new cleaning girl and right-hand man as she takes on changing my bed regularly and keeps my cupboards tidy – Jolly Good.

She is studying for a degree. Due to her high intelligence, she will pass, however I teach her how I think studying should work -
Some people study, study, study and still can't remember every word of what they are trying to learn.

Best study for, say 1.5 hours and then spend 0.5 hours thinking about something happy. Repeat 4 or 5 times.

During the 0.5 hours we know now that the brain moves the input from short term memory to long term memory. You will never forget what you've learned.

I have never failed an exam since I learnt this 66 years ago.

During April 2021 1 billion (1,000,000,000) vaccine doses have been injected into people's arms (about one seventh of the World's population of 7.78 billion people).

Some, in my view, untrusting types are refusing inoculation. All those who opt for no medical treatment (vaccination) should be left at home to die, although maybe, should receive paracetamol.

The non-vaccinated filled hospital beds resulting in my kidney cancer operation being delayed for 1 year. Hence my bias!

2022

The population of the World hits about 8.0 billion soles (latest figure available is 7,655,957,369 at one point in time in 2018).

FUTURE FORECASTS

Supermarkets in UK instructed to plan their ordering to ensure minimum food is wasted.

Farmers to decide size of vegetables to be delivered to supermarket. Supermarkets now have little control over what they sell.

Britain is the most significant trader in the Western World save China and India.

People born in 70's now expected to live to 140 years old, those born in 40's and 50's expected to live to 105 years old.

New laws passed to limit use of artificial intelligence.

80% of all cars electric.

UK now suffering regular power cuts as power generation is insufficient to replace the energy no longer available from petrol and diesel.

Fuel oil now outlawed for home heating.

UK begs World to follow suit.

EU in serious financial trouble.

Revolt against EU method of appointing important Heads of Departments, Judges, Officers without free elections.

Euthanasia is legal.

Western Countries issue edict to make it an offence to kill insects.

Insect species especially useful for plant pollination carries 1 year jail if killed.

Gas usage in UK diminishing since tax of 25% applied to bills.

UK now recovered from Brexit and on path to an incredible growth path in services and manufacturing.

Cannabis now legalised and smoked in cannabis cafes.

Global warming now realised by USA, China, and other large countries.

Artic and Antarctica ice melting shown 24/7 on ice loss T.V. channels.

2028

BBC disbanded. Other channels purchase popular programmes. All TV free.

Manufacture of non-compostable plastic components illegal. World Government issues tree planting programme.

Any non-zero carbon projects to compensate by 50 x carbon absorbing planting.

2030

EU converted to trading arrangement only. Virtually all diseases cured or managed.

Western countries people now living to 120 years of age. Discussion regarding limiting the length of life. Only 'useful' lives allowed to live beyond 110 years.

Colonisation of planet Mars commenced. Science now confirms that we are alone in the Universe.

The future of home heating almost certainly by 2038, gas as we know it will be banned but prior to this perhaps 2030. Hydrogen will be the main fuel, first by mixing it with our natural gas – this is illegal currently, the hydrogen must not exceed 0.1% of the total gas volume although 20% is actually safe. This will be a good start to changing over to 100% hydrogen. In 5 years', time boilers and stoves will be available known as "hydrogen ready" – requiring a quick change over from natural gas to hydrogen when this comes. There are about 2.5 million domestic boilers in the U.K. and the carbon dioxide saved by converting to hydrogen could be enormous.

Currently we use about 250 Tera Watt hours of gas per year (250,000,000,000/kilowatt-hours/year). (Tera = Trillion)

There is no way electricity could replace this. The idea of restricting houses from natural gas (said to be in 2038) is nonsense unless we start building thousands of windmills/tidal plants now and upgrade 70 to 80% of the national distribution grid, the overall cost is eye watering. Back up will have to be hydrogen mix.

The foregoing will not apply to new housing.

Today few new houses have a gas supply relying on electricity which can be generated distant from the homeowner by a high proportion (and soon 100% for most of the time) of renewable sources such as wind, tide, photovoltaic i.e., zero carbon.

This escapes the possibility of a tax on gas and the possibility of using heat pumps operating at a cost of some 20% to 30% of the basic cost of electricity – i.e., if the basic cost is 14 pence per kWh unit you pay 4 or 5p per unit of energy produced.

However, passive design may become required or wanted. This would require houses to be built totally airtight (no overflows poking through walls for example). Walls would include 300 mm (12") of insulation and 3 pane windows; gas filled will be a minimum requirement.

Ventilation will be much the same as now – small ducts supplying air to habitable rooms and any heat available in the extracted air used to warm the incoming air.

The only heating required beyond body heat (typically 113 watts per person) would be a micro heater situated in the supply air duct for use in the coldest weather. This high insulation proposal is often referred to as passive stancherd – in Germany it is called passivhaus and this name may catch on.

A new type of battery will become available with something like one thousandths the volume per Watt capacity – a battery for a mobile phone being 5 mm cubed. All homes will be served by battery power. The batteries being charged from fuel cells or hydrogen generator units.

The combination of hydrogen and micro batteries will pave the way for electric aircraft – giving quiet green flying.

2035

Gas is no longer available for house heating. Fuel cells now popular with gas grid (where possible) now carrying hydrogen.

Artificial intelligence now controlling some of what used to be called companies.

Teleportation is being tried with animals. The idea is to convert matter into energy (very small micro amounts), send by wire and then reassembled. Governments are spending Billions of Dollars and Pounds on this technique.

Brain to Brain communication commencing.

Plans now afoot to switch entire gas grids to Hydrogen.

2040

Working is not necessary except for pleasure. Governments pay an allowance to population that prefers not to work.

2045

Teletransportation now becoming available.

World Government agreed and concentrating on maintaining lower population.

New fusion energy used to split water into Oxygen Hydrogen – Oxygen released into atmosphere to maintain 24% Hydrogen distributed as fuel.

2047

My death as forecast by witch doctor in Zulu land.

2050

Communication brain to brain now possible. World Authority has data on all persons.

Artificial intelligence equipment can now converse between themselves Very little work undertaken by humans. 90% of population paid an allowance from the Government.

Pleasure grounds now popular. Sex dolls very popular, both male and female. These are now more popular than human sex partners.

There is now grid electricity only available to those licenced to use it.

Cash is no longer legal tender.

Most people live to 110 years or more.

Other than specific cases sex for reproduction is no longer allowed as it is necessary to reduce the population of the Planet.

Religious factors are heavily discussed. Licence to breed

available.

Sexual pleasure now limited to 'in brain sensation' – no physical relationship needed or wanted.

2075

Most pleasure is virtual even sex dolls no longer legal. Virtual sex now the norm.

2100

Humans can no longer converse with robots with artificial intelligence.

Robots accepted as a higher authority. Hymns and Prayers being developed to converse between robots and humans. Population of Mars now 1 million persons. Artificial intelligence not permitted on planet Mars. Robots don't have what us humans call consciousness.

APPENDICES

Appendix 1

Heat Pumps

There are several types but only 3 are of interest to us. The three are based on where they get their low-grade heat from:

The earth by burying pipes under or alongside the building where the temperature is a little higher than at the surface known as Ground Source Heat Pumps.

From underground water such as an aquafer.

From the air as is used in motor car air conditioning known as Air Source Heat Pumps.

A domestic refrigerator at home sits quietly until you put something into it that needs cooling – say a lump of cheese.

As the cheese is cooled, heat is given off and out of the back (or side) of the fridge.

The energy out of the back of your fridge can be 4 times the energy used to run the compressor that does the cooling. So why not a giant fridge and a giant block of cheese? As this is difficult instead of cooling down cheese let's cool down the earth beneath or alongside our building – this is what we do and now it's called ground source heat pump

In the summer we can literally reverse the system and cool the air (air conditioning) and warm the earth under our building – making it warmer for next winter's extraction – clever isn't it.

Appendix 2

Combined Heat and Power

This sexy title appeals to those who do not know about this system IN DETAIL.

The idea is to install a generator to produce single and three phase AC for general electric use and harvest the heat in the exhaust to use as general heating by warming water that can be delivered to radiators, under floor heating or other use such as hot water.

I will exaggerate to demonstrate. Let's assume we required 100 kW of electricity and 200 kW of heating. What shall we install? Let's say we install a unit to give 200 kW of heating and let's say it is a 200-kW generator.

Now, one September evening we need 10 lights on – so we start a 200,000-Watt, 200 kW generator and use 600 Watts - not good sense as we are going to waste all the heating and most of the electricity. Later we may require 100 kW of electricity but no heating (or hot water) so we are going to generate 200 kW of power but only use 100 kW and all the heat is wasted.

These systems are only green if the electric and heating loads are carefully balanced and switched in and out of a national grid supply.

There are some States in the USA where it is illegal (or against by-laws) to install these systems over 10 kW size due to the POSSIBLE waste of energy.

This system cannot be reversed to give a cooling installation. Most modern larger houses use heat pumps and virtually all commercial properties.

For some unexplained reason the new Addlestone shopping development is fitted with a combined heat and power unit plus several old-fashioned boilers. I wrote to the Chief Executive saying that the proposed design was de facto wrong.

He didn't agree. At the time of writing most shops are empty – they have to install and pay fully for their air conditioning – unbelievable!

Appendix 3

Building Regulations

As a fellow of the Chartered Institute of Building Services Engineers I take an interest in energy use and environmental pollution including global warming.

It is quite amazing that our building regulations do very little to reduce energy use and selection of fuel type.

As far as the insulation of houses is concerned, we have a series of Codes, Numbers 3, 4 being most popular. Code 4 gives requirements which are now normally worked to giving better results than our old-fashioned building regulation – why are our building regulations always behind general thinking?

As mentioned, our own Runnymede Council has installed gas fired boilers plus a small Total Heat and Power System (which emits carbon dioxide just like gas boilers). The whole system is environmentally unfriendly as far as our local area is concerned.

As mentioned, I wrote to the Chief Executive before the systems were finally designed explaining that such systems incorporate zero provision for cooling. I pointed out that in 20- or 30-years' time I would suggest even small dwellings will require some air cooling resulting in numerous boxes on external walls instead of a simple 2 pipes under the ground. Heat pumps should be incorporated using electricity but obtaining up to 4 times the heat that is paid for.

With the increasing use of renewable energy generating capacity such as wave and tide energy. The pollution caused by central generation is reducing, but our gas boilers and CHP system will continue to emit 500,000 tons of carbon dioxide per year until a new system is installed.

Undress to feel warmer!

Modern new larger houses with larger rooms often incorporate a small room, perhaps with a T.V. and Sofa called a snug. Such small rooms are often situated in the centre of the house with no direct window but have a direct connection to other rooms to meet the necessary Regulations. The heat losses from such a room and therefore the heat to be provided is often 120 watts or even less. Several years ago two light bulbs would provide sufficient heating – with modern lamps sufficient heating effect is not possible.

However, one person in light clothing will give off 115 watts of heat. By dispensing with the insulating effect of clothing this figure can rise to 135 watts.

So, if you are not warm enough take some clothes off!

(The T.V. will actually keep the room warm and a Labrador size dog will give off about 80 watts and a chicken 12 watts. A hamster will not help much giving off only 2 watts).

Appendix 4

Some more shipping lights

Small boats should show a green light on the right-hand side (called star board side) and a red light on the left-hand side (called port side) and a white light at the back (called the stern).

If the boat is a very small rowing boat like a little rubber blow up dinghy – best not go out at night but if you must, wave a torch around to prevent a collision.

If you are in a boat with divers down below you should know what to do. If you come across a small boat with a blue and white flag which is not moving and on a stick 1 metre high this means the boat is looking after a diver under the water. (The boat owner will call the stick a flagpole or a mast).

If you see a boat less than 20 metres long and has a washing basket hanging in its rigging during the day, this does not mean the Captain's wife want help with her washing, it means the boat is trawling for fish – keep well away.

Nevertheless, DON'T GO OUT SAILING ESPECIALLY IN THE DARK UNLESS YOU KNOW EXACTLY WHAT YOU ARE DOING.

Appendix 5

Politics

I have been associated with the Conservative Party since I was 23 – over 50 years and a full member of the Conservative Association for about 30 years.

This was the only party to vote for and over the years I have helped many people win a Councillor seat and become Chairman of local branches. Unfortunately for some unexplained reason the Party at National level now purposely opposes the wish of the general public.

For instance, recently:

We don't want War Boys freed from jail – can't be done, he must be freed (a private person arranged for him to stay in prison)
We want Afghanistan translators brought back urgently – can't be done
We want everybody caught carrying a knife to receive the sentences prescribed of 4 years in prison – can't be done

We want to leave the EU – can't be done

Sergeant Blackman arrested for murder and imprisoned for shooting the enemy. Yet drone operators in this country are killing the enemy in the Middle East – the operators are not in danger from the enemy so I guess they should be arrested for murder – can't be done.

Soldiers are taken to Court for shooting the enemy. At local level: The local branches to select candidates and run things – can't be done, the executive is boss

Branch membership cards to be locally issued and paid for locally, no longer can be done (it now takes 28 days to receive your card and the money that Branches used to be sent to HQ is now taken first by HQ making it look as though the Branch has brought in less cash)

Now need 15 members to agree a candidate – better if it's 6 or 8 –

can't be done the Executive has all power.

We are looking at the death of the Branches! Branches to die.

Appendix 6

Buddhism

You will have read of my direct experience of Buddhism when in Laos.

369 million people follow this religion or perhaps way of life, over 7% of the world's population.

As a comparison there are 2070 million people who follow the Christian way or about 6 times those who follow Buddhism.

It was founded by Gautama Buddha in India about 500 BC. It is a way of life based on peace and love.
The popular view of Buddhism conjures up mind pictures of Sharma shaven head monks wearing orange robes. This is a reasonable interpretation, but behind this is a dedicated religion composed of traditions, beliefs, and spiritual ways.

True Buddhist are the most peaceful and laid-back people on our planet. The big boss is The Dalai Lama who you will have seen on TV. More properly he is head of Tibetan Buddhism.

In my opinion, to sum up Buddhism, the followers concern themselves with the now. The past and future are not so important.

Appendix 7

The Farm I Worked On

We had a calf born with something wrong with its eyes – it was difficult to decide exactly what the problem was, but then Frank realised it was just cross eyed!

Apparently the ancient way of dealing with this is to, using a tube (plastic today) blow into the cow's bum and watch for its eyes to straighten.

I stood at the back with the tube and blew whilst Frank watched its eyes "STOP" he shouted – I had gone too far. "Oh dear" Frank said, "give me the tube and you watch". He pulled the tube out of the cows bum – I said, "why did you do that"? – he said, "well I'm not sucking the same end as you"!

Ted showed me how you can stroke a chicken (her neck) to make it go to sleep – more like a trance I thought. The idea was to then lay it down on the ground, stroke another one – lay that down and see how long a line of sleeping chickens could get. The winner was the one with the longest line and the loser had to sweep the yard.

Appendix 8

Good Value National Health

In 1960 I was working as a fitter's mate at a new school in Romford, Essex and, arriving one morning I watched as a helicopter was loaded with a guy or girl on a stretcher. Obviously, I guessed, going to Hospital after an accident.

Wow, the National Hearth Service has got everything covered – brilliant.

I am now 18, although I cannot remember how much I was earning, I do remember the tax and health insurance was taken out of my earnings as two distinct payments I'm sure the deduction for health was 7/6 per week (seven shillings and six pence) about 35 pence in our money.

Wow, I get all my medicines, operations and even helicopter evacuation for just 35 pence per week. I may have the figures wrong, but if health is shown separately one doesn't mind so such as to how much it is.

ODD AND SODS

Odds and Sods

Member World Pheasant Society

I was a member of the World Pheasant Society and was planning to breed rare and endangered species but first let's breed some more common species and I had 3 silver pheasants.

I had made 4 nest boxes – these are hidden under bushes in the aviary each by about 10" wide, 12" high and 30" long. The front (10" x 12") being only 50% enclosed for entry.

Wow, I came home from work, as usual went to see the pheasants and saw a pheasant egg on the aviary floor!

Exceptional excitement – went into the aviary and there was another just inside the door – but none in the next boxes. Altogether I found 10 eggs – this is not possible in one day.

It turned out that my wife Yvonne had visited a butcher who we used to use who also specialised in game.

She found the butcher about to throw away a tray of pheasant eggs. You guess the rest!!

Pheasants are bad mums and dads, and you need some broody (sexy) bantams to sit on the pheasant eggs.

To get the bantams broody (really to sit on eggs) we had to have a male bantam called a cockerel.

These crow and can wake everybody up at 5.00 in the morning – not popular. Yvonne's neighbour asked to see me to complain about the noise – I apologised and explained I ordered a 9.00 a.m. cockerel, but they sent me a 5.00 a.m. cockerel. As I cannot find a 9.00 a.m. one, I have ordered a mid-day one, and by crossing it I should get a 9.00 a.m. one. She said she thought I was so clever and looked forward to the result.

Same sex marriage comes to mind.

I find many people do not know why we clink glasses when toasting or simply say cheers. Well, assuming you have a nice white wine you probably realise:

It looks good
It feels good to hold
It smells wonderful
It tastes fantastic
CLINK
It sounds good

All five senses now satisfied.

If you meet somebody who thinks they know about the English Language – ask them: -
Which is correct – the Yoke of the EGGS IS white or the Yoke of the EGGS ARE white.

I will leave you to work it out.

A friend of mine, Doug, whilst on holiday in the country opened his car door just as another car passed close by and badly damaged the door – it was lucky his arm was not damaged.

On his return to work he told us about this and added "from now on I look in the mirror before I open the door!

I advised recently that the removal or abandonment of the gas installation in Runnymede Council's only tower block should be considered following being informed of a gas leak.

The reply suggested I should not listen to rumours and in any case the leak was very minor!

VERY MINOR! – Any gas leak should generate a total in-depth survey of the entire installation – why would one small area leak and no other small areas?

A minor leak can be more dangerous than a major leak – a large leak will be detected by smell and urgently dealt with. A minor leak in a relatively sealed area may not.
A 5% mix gas to air is explosive.

Other Points of Interest

Black Friday (shops cut prices)

This is a nonsense idea; I heard about it and was running out of sugar. I purposely held off buying any until Black Friday.

This Friday I went to Tesco's only to find sugar was the same price as before! I was given to understand everything was cheaper.

I arrived at Woking Station without a pen to do my crossword – no problem buy a pen at the paper kiosk. The shopkeeper said she only had these at 25 pence – fine, no problem.

Well, it wouldn't work, wow, I was very irritated and made a point of complaining the next morning – she simply said – well what do you expect for 25 pence – have I missed something?

Shakespeare had trouble choosing a pencil to write his plays with. He kept saying 2B or not 2B. Apparently he ended up with a B and when that went blunt he had an HB.

Science can be fascinating. I wore my watch on my left wrist but when I look in the mirror, the guy I look at is wearing his watch on his right wrist – amazing! Left goes to right and right goes to left. Why does this switch work sideways but not up and down?

I know this as when I wriggle my toes my ears do not move.

I also lay on the floor and again there was no switch of feet and head – very strange.

If you look in your driving mirror you will notice that the cars behind you are all left-hand drive – I guess they are getting ready for us leaving the EU.
The EU makes things very clear: The Lord's Prayer has 56 words
The Ten Commandments – 297 words
The American Declaration of Independence – 300 words The EU Directive on importation of duct eggs – 26,911 words

Is this clear? (numbers approximate)

A few definitions <u>Expert</u>

Expert is a two-part word consisting of EX and SPURT.

Now EX means gone, past as in Ex-Chairman – last year's Chairman – yesterday's person, old.

SPURT is a drip under pressure. So, an expert is an old drip working under pressure – not the best person to ask for advice.

<u>Barry's Way</u>

Barry's Way is a little-known road in Australia. It is the main road in Jindabyne in New South Wales, and you get to it via Snowy River road. You can, I think, follow it far enough and get to the NSW border with Victoria 76 km away. There is a lake at Jindabyne which I think is 915 m above sea level and close by there is a gin making brewery. The population is 2,629 living in 74% relative humidity.

Now it's in this book, I guess the town will become overcrowded. Fares from London are about £800 one way.

The opposite of not out is not in.

As a Councillor, I was paid an allowance which works out below the minimum wage – to get round this it is argued that a percentage of my work is as a volunteer – this part of the work is not paid for.

The payment is ridiculously low. I believe the external committee of, I think, 3 persons who agree the hourly/daily rate are selected by those who want the rate kept as low as possible.

We Councillors have no fixed hours of work, the maximum weekly time I have spent on Council work is 41 hours and the least is 0 per week.

I was interviewed by one such committee member during a week when I had spent 18 hours on council work. Incredibly he was not interested in the work I had done only on the time I spent in the Civic Office! Quite remarkable.

The method of agreeing rates are ridiculous and Runnymede are among the lowest in the country.

The Planning Committee and head of planning requires changing such that is if fit for purpose, I'll give you a few examples.

We desperately (we are told) require more housing.

Barrett's asked for planning for about 50 houses which were turned down by the Council and again after appeal, generally because they were in the opinion of the Officers and Committee too high. Unbelievable.

I think it was most unlikely that passers-by would come into the finished development and measure the height of the buildings. At the time, as an outsider I wanted to know why the planning officers did not phone Barratt and say – your buildings are too high instead they demanded Barrett's spend a further £15 to £20,000 on endless surveys including a whole week of bat surveys each night – I live near, I knew there were no bats. After this extra expenditure THEN the officers said 'your buildings are too high and therefore you cannot have planning permission.
The houses were attractively designed and not higher than the existing farmhouse other than the slope of the ground.

Very poor management.

I personally looked for planning for 9 houses – the officers said no – so we redesigned for 6, again the officers said no as the houses were up to 2 metres too close to the nearest village, 11 miles away!

It wasn't until a new officer, who had more brains, took over the project and recommended passing.

The processes, including a unilateral undertaking took several years and I lost my right to buy the site as our option agreement ran out. The Council could not care less.

Again, useless management. Head of planning and his team had no idea about the meaning of 'reasonable building'. They fit into my definition of 'EXPERT' (viz).

Surrey County Council also was not fit for purpose as far as planning is concerned. For some ancient reason roads and associated matters are decided by Surrey County Council not our local Runnymede Borough Council.

For many years the general public have heavily criticised the Council for not dealing with the road changes required to handle the new housing required. Even refusing to meet a delegation of residents who were invited to a meeting.

However, S.C.C. employed another external consultant who did not know what they were doing, having thought about the roads for 4 or 5 years, they design the worst roundabout I have ever come across. The design is as good as useless to reduce traffic problems. Most traffic is from the M25 to Woking – so what do they do – send it all round a new roundabout!

They purposely issued the design just a few weeks before a local election. The design was/is universally rejected as rubbish including building right over Ottershaw Car Park which is the centre of village activity, resulting in the existing Council seat holders being dismissed.

On contacting the leader of the Council pointing out the appalling design he claimed the design was only indicative!

I wonder why the Council's Consultant did not draw an elephant or something of interest.

Our tides are caused by the gravitational pull of the moon on the earth's water in the seas and oceans we are told.

The moon goes around the earth once per day but there are 2 high tides a day, why is this.

When giant computers came about I understand that the President of South Africa hired 3 of them, wired them together via the telephone system and asked this supercomputer "is God Black" – after going through endless formulas for 3 hours it punched out the answer "her colour is unknown".

I guess not everybody knows how to get a steam locomotive going.

Firstly, normally there is no ignition key, just a small door you open and light a fire inside. Make sure there is plenty of water in the boiler with the level showing more than halfway up the glass tube that indicates the water level, now sign up for lessons! It is far more complicated than you may think but when the water in the boiler boils and produces steam, one puts it in gear, eases the brake and then slightly opens the main steam valve then close it! Whilst closed the steam you have sent to the cylinders, cools very slightly, and expands and pushes the piston along, turning the wheels. If you had left the steam valve open you would have the equivalent of double what you want and probably got wheel spin! Then ease it open gently again and you are away. I haven't mentioned the other 39 things you should do.

It is illegal to drive a steam locomotive without a licence to do so and an apprenticeship to get one takes, I believe, 5 years.

I've decided, just after moving into the Farm, to put elephant powder down at each gate.

Some people ask why we do it – but it is remarkable stuff, we have had no trouble with elephants ever since we started so we are hesitant to stop doing this

Most ordinary matters that we live with every day exist as solid, liquid or gas (there is another state that doesn't affect us too much).

Water, for instance, is normally liquid – get it colder, it turns to ice, to get to a gas you have to heat it to 100°C.

So why do puddles dry up – they do not boil. I decided to write to the Minister in charge of the Department of the Environment to explain exactly what should be done about our flooding problem and my M.P. and chancellor of the Exchequer, Phillip Hammond was good enough to pass it on to her – an employee of the Department of the Environment phoned me to say my views fitted into the department's thinking. I asked if I was speaking to a scientist and the helpful lady said she was an engineering assistant. I asked her if she knew why puddles dry up – she said she wasn't sure if the department had an official view on this matter.

- So, what hope have they got to solve our flooding problems?

The livery company – The Worshipful Company of Felt makers of London held a Banquet at the Mansion House, 5 June. I attended with 11 guests. We ate off gold service. The reader may be interested in the menus.

Terrine of Vegetable Basil Mayonnaise	Muscadet St Clements 1985
Fillet of Sole Florentine White Wine Sauce	
Roast Rack of Lamb with Riz De Veau and Mushrooms	Chateau Haut Peyregent 1981
New Potatoes in their Skins Buttered Broccoli	
Fresh Pineapple in Calvados with Lemon Sorbet	Croft LBV
Coffee Petits Fours	Hennessey VSOP/Liqueurs

The toast to the Livery Company was given by the Lord Mayor of London.

The meal finished at about 9.00 'our ladies present declared "What" – I'm not going home yet it took me all day to get ready. Four of us took our limo to Beoty's Restaurant, sat in the window seat, and ordered a bottle of Moet and fried egg sandwiches with brown sauce.

I have never before or since eaten fried egg sandwiches in white tie and tails garb.

Jack Cohen

The Tesco owners tie motive YCMMSOYA stands for "you can't make money sitting on your arse". This was revealed after his death.

Planning and Our Council

The next 35 years.

I live in the Borough of Runnymede where the Magna Carter was signed by King John in 1215 on the 15th of June which gave the common person some basic rights and became the basis of many of our laws.

I am told that King John was quite a nice guy, and the important gentry and landowners were able to persuade (force?) him to sign some of the King's rights away and give them to the public.

Runnymede now is mainly controlled by the Local Council and the King has little direct authority.

The Council is a financial miracle. We are, I think, the Council with the 4th lowest rate of Council Tax in the Country and have never cut any services (many Councils have found it to be necessary to cut services from a financial point of view).

Our Corporate Head of Resources and Investing has an exceptional ability to keep the books in credit and money in the bank.

On the other hand, our planning department was, in my opinion, one of the worst in the Country. Indeed, our head of planning and his team has been putting together a proposed plan for the future of Runnymede for the next 35 years but only covers housing in any detail.

For some strange reason the Government suggest (force) that we build hundreds of cheap houses (so called Social housing) for all our homeless families which as far as I can see we haven't got.

As our team did not know where to propose houses, they employed an external Consultant, called ARUP, who, in my opinion, knew nothing about Runnymede. About 18/20 years ago I went to see the Council to discuss the future of the Borough and a very knowledgeable lady came to the planning counter (as the Council operated back then) and explained that the most significant future matter would be building about 400 houses on a site with access from the main M25 to Woking Road and the widening of this road. I got the impression that this was all planned out ready to be incorporated in the new plan to be put forward in 2015 (she said) – about 25 years' time then.

As a Councillor, I asked how this was going – the reply indicated that the Officers did not know what I was talking about. A senior officer stated with much clarity that independent consultants will calculate how many houses we should build and where they should go!

Amazing – what will they know about Runnymede?

They prepared a drawing. As it was not very clear I asked the Consultant to point out our Civic Centre – he got it quite wrong.

They plan cheap houses next to upmarket estates and caused an uprising of Runnymede residents.

I am informed that the silly way they calculate the number of houses required is recommended by the Government.

It is mathematically inaccurate!

Step 1 - guess how many required

Step 2 - as adjacent Boroughs will hear about the plan to build – the other Boroughs homeless and residents will apply to rent or buy

Step 3 - building more to cater for new interest

Step 4 - repeat step 2 and 3 three times

So, we are trying to solve an equation with two unknowns based on two variables (number of "homeless", number of houses required).

None of the proposed locations are liked by the residents.

Likewise, a plan has emerged to include one Gypsy/Traveller plot per location!

Why build in Runnymede anyway? Jump on a train to the North of England and you will pass thousands of acres of land where we can build new towns, following the successful developments at Milton Keynes and others.

I wouldn't be surprised if our submission fails. If this is the case the Council will hire more consultants who known nothing of Runnymede!

By the time you read this book you will know the outcome.

The external consultants, ARUP, who, in my opinion didn't know what they were doing as far as Runnymede is concerned suggested 10 sites to be taken out of the green belt for cheap housing, virtually all of them adjoining up- market established housing areas.

Believe it or not their first proposal was to build 8,939 cheap homes in our area or very close to it to include Fairoaks Airport.

At 2.2 persons per cheap house indicates just under 20,000 persons would be homeless if we do not build as suggested.

Rubbish.

Our head of planning and his team, the chairperson of the planning committee and the planning committee left it to Surrey County Council to consider the infrastructure required for this horrendous building proposal. The result is nothing was considered. The entire local population was quite correctly up in arms.

From what we – the public – heard no extra shops, doctor's surgeries, schools, roads were required!

Sailing a Boat at Sea

If you want to travel North at 5 knots (roughly 6.5 mph) and you know that the tide is travelling at 5 knots going to the East, in which direction will the boat try and go? Answer – Northeast. So, to get where you want to go you actually steer North West and the tide will actually take you North.

If you can't work this out and also allow for Magnetic Deviation and Magnetic Declination (sometimes referred to as variation, best hire a navigator (Deviation is the actual North compared with what the compass indicates as North). The up-to-date Admiralty Chart will tell you what to allow in the area you are sailing - maybe – 5°. It is different all over the planet depending on such things as depth of iron deposits under the earth's surface.

Don't assume travelling South is downhill all the way when you try to plot your course on a globe!

I have seen some strange things at sea and only 2 or 3 miles from the coast. The strangest is a circle of flat water some 30 feet diameter in an otherwise rough sea. This reminded me of crop circles.

What do you know about the E.U.

The following is strictly my view. I have already mentioned my mild dislike of fraudulent organisations, but do you realise that the E.U. with its 73 Members of the Parliament from Britain and a further 628 from other countries has never had its accounts signed off due (as far as I know) due to fraud.

As far as I can see the representatives from the 28 countries are encouraged (made?) to vote in favour of bills put forward by the executive controlled by Germany.

If a country were to vote against (veto) a bill they know that their annual grant from the E.U. will diminish, so nobody risks running against the wish of the bosses.

The latest figures I have to hand suggests the UK puts in €14,100,000,000 and takes out £7,000,000,000, Spain puts in €11,100,000,000 and takes out
€11,500,000,000, Germany puts in €29,900,000,000 and takes out €11,150,000,000.

I do not know who agrees with these figures, although I have only come across one case when our Margaret Thatcher kept them all talking well into the night to get the money she wanted.

How to Win Business Over Lunch.

Firstly, make sure your prospective Client sits opposite you and check there are plenty of "things" on the table such as glasses, dessert fork and spoon, and salt and pepper pots. Towards the end of the meal, it is not unusual to fiddle with the items on the table, pick up a salt container, but put it down a little closer to your Client.

Fiddle with everything you can and gradually keep your space clear and his cluttered. He will feel quite inferior when you say, 'so what plans have you regarding the contract I'm hoping to land".

Note – read her or him – I guess you would know who is opposite you!

I shall always remember attending St Peters Hospital for a pre-op examination. I was shown into a room containing a desk, 2 chairs and an examination 'couch'. The Nurse said, "lower your trousers and lay on the couch".

I said, "heavens that's quick I normally have to buy dinner". The Nurse laughed.
I need to write another book covering the EU, COVID Virus and Economy, maybe.

END

PHOTOGRAPHS

Where is James going?

JC catching tonight's supper

Antony teaching skiing to 2 at once

My new Italian suit 1961

Fighting our Spinnaker 1988 in my new shorts

Olly standing still for dear Romany!

Nearly there

Warship Forester is a big ship

Printed in Great Britain
by Amazon